The Prisoner

Nancy Rue

PUBLISHING
Colorado Springs, Colorado

Library of Congress Cataloging-in-Publication Data
Rue, Nancy N.
   The prisoner / Nancy Rue.
      p.   cm.   —   (Christian heritage series ; bk. 10)
   Summary: In the winter of 1781, with the Revolutionary War closing
in on Williamsburg, eleven-year-old Thomas Hutchinson must decide
how to handle his own battles with bullies at school and worries
about the Loyalist sympathies of his best friend's family.
   ISBN 1-56179-518-6
   1. Williamsburg (Va.)—History—Revolution, 1775–1783—Juvenile
fiction. [1. United States—History—Revolution, 1775–1783—
Fiction. 2. Williamsburg (Va.)—Fiction. 3. Christian life—
Fiction.] I. Title. II. Series: Rue, Nancy N. Christian heritage
series ; bk. 10.
PZ7.R88515Pr   1997   96-38992
[Fic]—dc21   CIP
                                                                  AC

Published by Focus on the Family Publishing,
Colorado Springs, Colorado 80995.
Distributed in the U.S.A. and Canada by Word Books, Dallas, Texas.

The author is represented by the literary agency of Alive Communications,
1465 Kelly Johnson Blvd., Suite 320, Colorado Springs, CO 80920.

This is a work of fiction, and any resemblance between the characters in this book
and real persons is coincidental.

Editor: Keith Wall
Cover Design: Bradley Lind
Cover Illustration: Cheri Bladholm

Printed in the United States of America

97 98 99 00/10 9 8 7 6 5 4 3 2 1

For the whole Rue clan,
whose name I am proud to bear.

A Map of
Williamsburg
1780–81

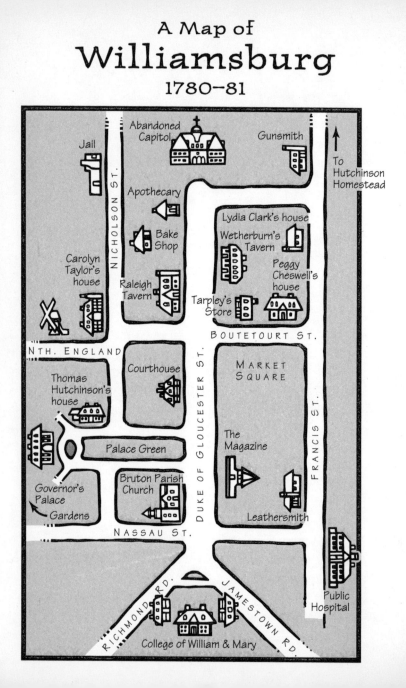

Chapter One

The snowball Malcolm Donaldson hurled from behind the powder magazine hit Thomas Hutchinson square in the face. It broke into slushy chunks that drizzled all the way from his deep-set blue eyes to his square, young jaw.

Thomas grinned as he scooped up a handful of snow and hurled it back. It connected right in the middle of the Scottish servant boy's back.

"I got you, Malcolm!" he cried. "You aren't so mighty now!"

"Don't worry, Tireless! I'll get you back!"

Malcolm let go with a barrage of icy balls that plastered Thomas everywhere from the cap that covered his tangle of black hair to the clunky boots that were ankle-deep in the rare Virginia snow. Thomas ignored the fact that his cheeks

1

and hands were so cold he couldn't feel them anymore and returned fire with a peppering from his own stack of ammunition.

The British army—those lousy Redcoats—they have nothing on me! he thought happily as he took a hit in the ear and then evened the score with a blow to Malcolm's forehead. *I'll have Malcolm buried in the time it would take them to load their guns.*

Malcolm had made his fort next to the magazine, the six-sided building where the Patriots kept their weapons and ammunition for the War for Independence—and he ducked behind it now. *Probably to make some more "musket balls,"* Thomas told himself. *I might as well make a few more myself, just in case he isn't ready to surrender yet.*

He leaned over to gather up more snow and stopped for a second to admire the way the sun sparkled on it. The winter of 1781 was going to make history, not just because there was a war with England going on in nearby North and South Carolina, but also because there were six inches of snow on the ground. It almost never snowed in Williamsburg, Virginia, and Thomas was going to enjoy every flake of it.

He was just appreciating the way it squeaked under his wool-clad fingers when something hit him, hard, on the seat of his breeches. He caught his balance—no small feat for an 11-year-old who was as big as 15-year-old Malcolm—and whirled to look behind him. A hand was just disappearing behind an abandoned market wagon.

Malcolm? he thought. *How did he get behind me?*

A snowball sailed at him from the magazine then, splashing to bits on his shoulder. Malcolm was still there. The snowball that had gotten Thomas in the tail had come from somebody else's hand. Thomas burrowed behind his tree stump and watched.

There was a long pause. *They're all holding their fire,* Thomas thought. That was a soldier's term his older brother Sam had taught him before he'd gone off to fight in the war. But slowly, a black-capped head appeared above the wagon, and beside it another one.

Who are those two boys? Thomas wondered. Since he'd moved to Williamsburg from the Hutchinsons' plantation near Yorktown last spring, he'd met almost everyone in town. That was easy to do, making deliveries every afternoon for Francis Pickering, the apothecary. But he'd never seen these two small boys before.

Just then their heads rose higher, and Thomas blinked. Why were they wearing masks over the lower half of their faces? It was a wet-cold day, but not cold enough to have to cover your nose.

Wait a minute, Thomas thought suddenly. *I've seen masks like that! Could that be—?*

But before he could finish his thought, Malcolm skidded into the snow beside him, pointing toward the wagon.

"We have company," he said, his sharp black eyes alive with mischief. "Shall we take them on together?"

Thomas felt an impish idea creep into his head. "Do you know who they are?"

Malcolm shook his dark, shaggy head.

"All right, then," Thomas said. "I say we can make them surrender in five snowballs."

"Four," Malcolm said.

Malcolm always had to have the last word, but Thomas just nodded and packed a globe of snow into his hand. "After you," he said.

Malcolm smiled his square smile, rose to his knees, and heaved a snowball at the bigger of the two black caps. It collided with the wearer's head and knocked the boy backward into the snow.

"One down," he said smugly. "Your go."

Thomas didn't launch his quite so hard, though he could have with his big Hutchinson arm. He knew who he was aiming at, and it wouldn't do to be too rough. The snowball hit the top of the other cap with a soft plump.

"We'll never take them that way!" Malcolm chided him. He pulled his arm back. "Watch how it's done, lad."

But the snowball had barely left his hand when the two caps disappeared and then reappeared under the wagon.

"They're going to give up already," Malcolm whispered. "Let's go for a head-on attack."

Thomas stifled a snort and nodded. "I'll follow you," he said.

Malcolm crawled out from behind the stump on his belly and slithered like a snow snake across the frosted ground. Thomas stayed behind and put his hand over his mouth to keep from guffawing out loud.

Malcolm was only a few yards from the wagon when the two bodies underneath it sprang to life and were on him. One giggled. The other shrieked. Both of them rolled

Malcolm first to one side and then the other, shoving snow inside his shirt and vest as if they were stuffing a turkey.

"Stop, lads, or I shall have to hurt you both!" Malcolm shouted.

One did stop and stood up, reaching inside his bulky coat and pulling something out. When Thomas saw what it was, he couldn't hold back the laughter any longer.

"Get him, Martha!" one of the attackers cried.

But Martha didn't—much to Malcolm's good fortune. Martha was a fat orange cat that on a warmer day would gladly have scratched both of Malcolm's cheeks to ribbons. But it was far too cold for a cat with her comfortable tastes. She gave a low growl and climbed back inside the boy's shirt, while the other boy continued to roll on the ground with Malcolm, sending snow flying in all directions.

Only neither one of them was a boy. Malcolm found that out when he finally reached up and pulled the mask off the little tiger who was working at pinning his arms down. A pair of green eyes twinkled down at him, with one tiny dimple in each cheek.

"Patsy!" Malcolm cried. He yanked off her cap, and two dark-brown braids popped merrily out. "My own sister!"

The other "boy" tried to make a dash in the direction of the courthouse, and Thomas scrambled up and took off after her. Caroline Taylor could run like a deer on dry ground, but she was no match for the Hutchinson "log legs" in the snow. In three strides, the mask and cap were off, exposing sandy-blond hair, dancing brown eyes, and two ruddy cheeks covered with what looked like a thousand dimples.

"Impostor!" Thomas cried.

"Scoundrel!" she cried back. "We had you both fooled!"

Malcolm joined them with 10-year-old Patsy flung across his back. Her mouth, full of charmingly crooked teeth, was grinning.

"You knew all the time it was them!" Malcolm said to Thomas.

Thomas grinned and said, "No!"

"You lie like a hearth rug, Thomas," Caroline said, hands on the hips of her too-big brown woolen breeches.

"Where did you get those pants?" he asked. "Out of Alexander's closet?"

As soon as the words left his mouth, Thomas wanted to snatch them back, but it was too late. The sparkle left Caroline's eyes, and she looked down at the toes of her boots, which were also probably her big brother's.

Ever since Alexander Taylor had disappeared last fall, the mere mention of his name was enough to put Caroline in the doldrums. It wasn't so much that he had left Williamsburg, just as Thomas's brother Sam had. It was the fact that no one knew for sure whether he had run off to spy for the British and Loyalists—people like his father, Robert Taylor, the miller, who thought everyone should remain loyal to the king—or whether he had become a Patriot like the Hutchinsons and was fighting for independence.

Thomas didn't care which side Caroline was on. Even though she was a girl, she was his best friend, and that was all that counted. But lately, talk of Alexander made him wonder if she felt the same way.

"You'll be wantin' to take your boot out of your mouth now, lad," Malcolm muttered close to his ear.

Thomas pulled away and shoveled up a handful of snow. "This battle isn't over!" he shouted. "Come on, then. Caroline and I against the Donaldsons!"

"All right, if you two poor blighters are willing to lose!" Malcolm said, grinning squarely.

Patsy squealed and squirmed down from his shoulders.

Even Caroline dimpled a little. "Who are you calling blighters, Malcolm?" Then she turned and said, "Come on, Tom, let's take them, eh?"

She stuck her black cap over her hair again and danced off toward the wagon with Thomas on her heels. She coaxed a disgruntled Martha out of her coat and into the broken wagon bed and then squatted down beside Thomas. They'd only begun to make their pile of snowy cannonballs when the wintry air was pierced by the blast of a horn. Caroline and Thomas both stiffened.

"Is that the post rider, do you think?" Caroline asked.

The horn bleated again, and this time Thomas heard the clop of hooves along with it. "It's sure it is," he said.

They climbed up into the rickety old wagon and watched as a man with a wind-whipped face trotted down the Duke of Gloucester Street on a horse with a wide leather bag secured behind its saddle. Once again he cocked his leather-capped head back and announced his arrival with a long blow of the brass post horn he carried in one hand. The tails of his red watch coat flapped up and down as he passed, and they knew he was on his way to the print shop, where the printer would receive the mail for the citizens of Williamsburg and pass it out.

Thomas cast a sideways glance at Caroline. She watched until the big leather post bag disappeared inside the shop. *She's wondering if there's word from Alexander in there,* he decided. He felt a pang jab at his insides. He would like to know what had happened to Alexander Taylor, too. Ever since last spring, Alexander had been Thomas's teacher— and his friend. Thomas missed him as much as he missed Sam. There could never be another teacher like him, and Thomas's father seemed to know it, too. So far he hadn't made other arrangements for his education, and that was fine with Thomas. He loved working in Francis Pickering's apothecary shop. He'd be content to be an apprentice for Francis and Dr. Nicholas Quincy forever.

There was a loud, between-the-fingers whistle from behind the powder magazine. "Will we be havin' this battle today or not?" Malcolm called.

"You're anxious to get beaten, then?" Thomas hollered.

He jumped down from the wagon, and a moment later, Caroline joined him. She was trying to smile.

"Let's give them the battle of their lives, Tom," she said.

Thomas wasn't sure how many battles the Donaldsons had actually seen, though Malcolm read everything he could get his hands on about the war. He often explained things to the rest of the Fearsome Foursome about the tactics of the Americans' General Washington and the British commander in the south, General Cornwallis. He even understood about Benedict Arnold, the Patriot traitor who was now fighting for the British. But none of them had ever seen a battle, because the war still hadn't come to Virginia. Thomas thought Malcolm secretly wished it would.

"Ready?" Caroline hissed. "Aim . . . fire!"

Thomas let fly with three snowballs, one right after the other, and then ducked before Malcolm's well-aimed missiles could get him in the face. Caroline squealed as she took one of Patsy's in the nose.

"Tom," she said, tugging at his sleeve. "I'm going to sneak up into the wagon where I can get better aim. Distract them."

Thomas saluted and then crept behind a wheel. He whipped off his cap and tossed it out into the snow, and at once one of Patsy's snowballs flew in that direction. Thomas dashed out to retrieve his hat, dodging three of Malcolm's hard-thrown bullets in the process. Nobody could throw harder than wiry Malcolm. Thomas laughed out loud as he dove under the wagon and felt it rock with Caroline's movement. She should be setting up her shots right about now. He held his breath and waited.

But it wasn't the surprised shouts of Malcolm or the delighted giggles of little Patsy that he heard. Instead, a scream shot out from above him—a Caroline scream that went right through him.

"What's wrong?" he whispered hoarsely.

"Tom!" she cried, in a voice that went through him. "Tom, I'm bleeding!"

✛ ⬥ ✛

Chapter Two

Thomas hauled himself into the wagon just as Malcolm, too, was vaulting over the side. Patsy climbed up onto one of the wheels, her eyes as wide as a pair of pewter plates.

"Did you say you were bleeding, lass?" Malcolm asked.

But from where Thomas stood, he could see it already. Globs of red were spurting from between the fingers Caroline was holding to her forehead.

"What happened?" Thomas cried.

"I got hit—with a snowball—"

At once, anger sizzled up the back of Thomas's neck. "Why did you have to throw so hard, Malcolm?"

"Don't be a fool, lad." Malcolm picked something up from the bottom of the wagon. "That was no snowball. It was a rock, covered with snow."

Thomas snatched it from him and stared at it. It was as big as his fist with sharp points sticking out. "Who threw this?" he said.

Malcolm scanned the Market Square and courthouse yard with his sharp eyes narrowed into a fierce glare. No one could look quite as menacing as Malcolm. Thomas always thought it must be from all those years of thieving with his father in Scotland before he was sent to America. Right now the dangerous eyes seemed to snag on something, and Malcolm thrust out a pointing finger.

"There!" he cried.

Thomas turned and saw it, too—three young male figures peering out from behind the stocks and pillory.

"You there!" Malcolm called. "Did you throw that rock?"

Thomas, however, didn't wait for an answer. He leaped from the wagon like an attacking cat and charged at them.

"Bullies!" he yelled. "You'll pay for that!"

For an instant, the three boys froze. Even as Thomas careened toward them across the road, he formed a clear picture of them. The tallest one, who still wasn't as tall as Thomas, curled his lip as if he smelled something bad, revealing a gap between his two front teeth. To one side of him, a spongy boy with a wide face and even wider ears gaped with his lower lip hanging almost to his chin. To his other side, a good-looking, auburn-haired lad darted his eyes around, causing them to glint in the sun like pieces of silver.

It looked as if they were going to wait like a trio of statues for Thomas to spring on them. But as he hurtled forward,

Thomas's boot slid on a patch of ice. His legs skittered out from under him, and he groped the air with flailing arms until he was flat on his stomach in the snow. The three boys wasted no time bursting into a chorus of screaming laughter.

"Clumsy oaf!" the tallest one cried.

"Yes, clumsy!" said the one with ears like open carriage doors.

Thomas tried to scramble up, but he only lost his footing again and dug his chin into the snow. The boy with the silver eyes kicked a spray of flakes into Thomas's face and shrieked.

"Swine!" Thomas cried.

Behind him he heard footsteps crunching toward him and felt a set of wiry fingers curl around his collar. The three boys scattered like startled chickens and were gone.

Thomas tried to wriggle away as Malcolm got him to his feet. "I have to go after them!"

"No. We have to get Caroline home! She's hurt bad, lad."

Only then did Thomas see Caroline behind Malcolm, leaning on Patsy and still bleeding through her fingers. The three boys dissolved from Thomas's mind. He had been at Dr. Quincy's side when he'd taken care of bleeding patients. He knew the doctor should be there.

"Get Nicholas, Patsy!" he cried. "Hurry!"

Malcolm nodded to his little sister, and she took off like a musket ball toward Francis Pickering's apothecary shop, where the doctor usually could be found when he wasn't out tending to someone's aliments. Without Patsy to lean on,

Caroline wobbled unsteadily, and Malcolm scooped her up.

"I'll run ahead and tell Mistress Betsy!" Thomas said, and he bolted toward Nicholson Street and the Taylors' house. *"You have to stop them from bleeding before they faint dead away,"* he could hear Nicholas Quincy instructing him. And he could almost hear Nicholas starting to pray the way he always did over his patients. Just as he had learned to do last fall, Thomas started a prayer of his own.

"Please, God," he said out loud. "Don't let her faint dead away."

Caroline didn't "faint dead away," and within minutes of Nicholas's arrival at the Taylors', he had the wound cleaned and bandaged and bee balm tea ordered from Caroline's mama, Betsy.

"I'm usually the one lying in bed with the doctor looking down at me," frail Betsy said as she set the tray on the cherry-wood drop-leaf table in Caroline's room. "And I'd give anything if it were me this time!"

"Not to worry, Mistress Betsy," Nicholas said as he packed up his bag. "If she rests well tonight, she'll be up and about tomorrow, throwing snowballs again."

"But not rocks!" Betsy said. "Who would do such a thing?"

All eyes turned to Thomas. Although Malcolm and Patsy were there in Caroline's red-and-white flowered room, they didn't say a word. As servants, they didn't speak unless spoken to, especially in other people's houses.

"It was three boys," Thomas said. "I'd never seen them before."

"That isn't surprising," Caroline's mother said. "Ever since last week, strangers have been pouring into Williamsburg from homes all along the river and taking up residence wherever they can find a place. I went to the milliner's shop today, and there were saddle horses tied all along the hitching bars." She shook her head. "I've not seen it this way since the capital was here, before Governor Jefferson left for Richmond."

Thomas had often heard his father talk about those years when Williamsburg bustled with the excitement of men like Patrick Henry and Thomas Jefferson. But now it was a sleepy little town.

I wonder why it's waking up? Thomas thought.

There was no time to ask, though, because Caroline's door flew open and Robert Taylor burst in. He was always a serious man—Thomas wasn't sure he'd ever seen him smile—but his face was drawn up tighter than ever as he hurried to Caroline's bed.

"I just saw Francis Pickering. He said she was hurt. What's happened? Is it bad?"

While Betsy tried to answer the questions that tumbled out of him one after another, Nicholas stood by looking suddenly awkward and farm-boyish. It always seemed strange to Thomas that the doctor looked as if he were in charge of the world when he was taking care of a sick person, but as soon as his work was done, the tall, thin, pale-eyed man slumped over as if he weren't quite sure what to do with his long arms and legs.

"Thomas!" Caroline whispered.

Thomas slipped to the bed and leaned over. Malcolm and Patsy scooted in, too.

"Why did those boys throw that rock at me?" she asked. "Do they know Papa's a Loyalist? Is that what it was?"

"How could they know that? They don't even live here," Malcolm said. "They're just young idiots is all."

Thomas felt the anger burning on the back of his neck again. "I don't care who they are! They're going to get it from me!"

Caroline frowned—and then winced. "No fighting, Tom. You know you always get in trouble when you fight."

Malcolm folded his arms across his chest. "Don't worry, Courageous," he said to Caroline. "I'll see he doesn't do anything stupid. Come on, Patsy, I'd best be gettin' you home to Mistress Lydia's."

Thomas scowled after Malcolm as he led his sister out to take her back to Lydia Clark, the young woman she worked for.

"Why are you looking that way, Tom?" Caroline said. "Malcolm's right, it is stupid to fight."

"I don't care!" Thomas whispered back. "He isn't my master—"

"That's wonderful news!" Betsy Taylor cried suddenly.

Caroline and Thomas left their own words in midair and looked at her. Her tiny mouse's face was glowing from within her halo of golden hair. Dr. Quincy stood next to her, looking awkward and excited at the same time.

"What's wonderful news, Mama?" Caroline asked.

Betsy pointed to a piece of paper in Robert Taylor's hand.

"Your father just picked up our mail from the printer's shop. We have a letter from Alexander!"

Thomas felt his eyes jump wide open. Caroline struggled to sit up in bed.

"What does it say?" she said.

"He's safe," said her father. "He doesn't say exactly where he is—but he says it isn't far away—and it's right where he belongs—with the British."

The faintest glimmer of a smile passed over his face, and just as quickly it clouded over. His serious eyes rested on Thomas.

"I would appreciate it if you would not mention this to anyone, young Hutchinson," he said. "It would only mean trouble for our family, and I would hate to see that after all your father has gone through to protect us. And you, too, Dr. Quincy. Please, not a word of this."

The doctor muttered, "Of course."

Thomas nodded as if he were numb. He wouldn't tell. Papa wouldn't either if he knew. It was John Hutchinson's job to protect the remaining Williamsburg Loyalists from Patriots who wanted to drive them out of town—or worse. But it wasn't that thought that had just stopped his heart in his chest.

It was that Alexander, his teacher and his friend, was really spying for the British against the Americans. Alexander was the one who had found a place for Sam in the American army and helped him get there. Alexander had told both Sam and Thomas that he was a Patriot now.

He had lied to them.

Caroline's parents went to the doorway and whispered excitedly to each other. Caroline propped herself up on her elbow and motioned to Thomas.

"You don't hate Alexander now, do you?" she asked in a low voice.

Thomas hunched his shoulders uncomfortably and glowered at the flowers on Caroline's bed hangings.

"You don't, do you?" she said again.

"No," Thomas blurted out in a hoarse whisper, "because it isn't true!"

"What do you mean?"

"Alexander isn't fighting for the British! He wouldn't lie to me. He wouldn't!"

"He wouldn't lie to Papa, either—"

"Yes, he would!"

Caroline bunched up her slice-of-melon mouth. "You can't have everything your way, Tom."

She might as well have slapped him, the words stung so hard. Thomas slowly backed away from the bed.

"There's no need to get all puffed up like a porcupine," she said. "Just because you're wrong."

"I'm not wrong!" he spat out at her.

He felt a hand on his shoulder then and looked up into Dr. Quincy's pale-blue eyes.

"Our patient needs her rest," he said.

Thomas didn't look back at her as he stomped out of the room.

✝ ✙ ✝

Chapter Three

As soon as he was out the front door, Thomas wanted to run back and have his conversation with Caroline over again.

I'm a stupid idiot! he screamed to himself. *Why did I talk so ugly to her?*

But he knew why. Because he couldn't stand the thought of Alexander working for the British. That would mean he had lied to Thomas. His beloved teacher had lied.

Thomas and Nicholas were halfway to the Hutchinsons' house on the Palace Green before he trusted himself to speak again.

"At least *you* haven't gone off to war," he said to Nicholas. "It's so confusing when people go and we don't know where they are."

"Or who they're fighting for?" Nicholas said softly. His

breath chugged out in frosty puffs as he looked down his cold, red nose at Thomas. "You've no need to worry about me, my friend. You'll remember I'm a Quaker. We don't believe in war."

In silence they passed the old Governor's Palace, the one that had been lived in by royal governors until the Declaration of Independence, and then by the two American governors, Patrick Henry and Thomas Jefferson. But now where chandeliers had once sparkled down on a ballroom full of glittering dancers, only a few candles guttered and spat in their holders, waiting for wounded soldiers to come to the makeshift hospital inside.

"If you *were* to go to war, would you work in a place like that?" Thomas asked.

Nicholas shook his head. "I want no part of war in any way. My calling from God is to serve the people of Williamsburg, and that is what I will do."

There was nothing farm-boyish in the way he said it.

Plenty of candles burned merrily in the Hutchinsons' house as Nicholas saw Thomas up the walk. The light burst out at them as tall, broad-shouldered John Hutchinson opened the front door and extended a big hand.

"Dr. Quincy!" he said in his deep voice. "Won't you join us for supper?"

"I wouldn't want to impose—"

"Nonsense! Virginia would be crushed for days if you didn't come in, and Clayton is here for a time. Surely you want to look in on him."

That did it, of course. Thomas's oldest brother Clayton had a weak heart and had almost died last fall. Nicholas was experimenting with ways to strengthen it, and he never missed a chance to see how the ailing Clayton was healing.

But what is Clayton doing here? Thomas wondered as he followed Nicholas into the cheery house. *He's supposed to be running the plantation so Papa can attend to the warships he's having built.* Thomas bristled. Clayton was his brother, but he wasn't Thomas's favorite person.

There was happy confusion in the dining room as Esther, the Hutchinsons' lifelong servant—*and family busybody,* Thomas always added in his mind—set a place for Nicholas and Malcolm stoked the fire and Thomas's mother fussed over the lot of them.

"What smells so good, Mistress Virginia?" the doctor asked politely.

Thomas sniffed. It *did* smell good. It couldn't be something Esther had concocted. She had always been a nurse to the children—even to Papa himself when he was a baby—and not a cook. That was very apparent in some of the things that appeared on the Hutchinsons' table.

"Rabbit stew," said Mama. "It's so hard to get any other meat, what with the war going on."

"Compliments of our Malcolm Donaldson," Papa put in. "He caught the rabbit and showed Esther how to prepare it."

"That would explain it," Clayton mumbled.

Thomas let his mouth water and hungrily eyed the tureen Papa was dipping the ladle into.

"My question," Nicholas said, "is what brings you to town, Clayton?"

The cheeriness of the cozy dining room suddenly disappeared as if it had been snapped out by a pair of fingers. A shadow passed over John Hutchinson's face.

"I'm afraid it's bad news that brings him here," Papa answered. "You know the name Benedict Arnold, I'm sure."

There was a general nodding around the table.

"Last month, he landed 1,200 British soldiers in Hampton, seized all the small craft he could find, and has begun to sail up the James River. He's wreaking havoc and destruction all along the way."

"What do you mean, John?" Mama asked nervously.

Papa studied his stew for a moment. "You know the Berkeley Plantation?"

"That's Benjamin Harrison's place, isn't it?" Nicholas said.

"It is. One of Virginia's finest statesmen. Arnold's men went into the house, took out all the family portraits, and burned them on the front lawn."

"How dreadful!" Mama cried. Her black curls trembled around the rim of her lacy cap.

"What on earth is the sense in that?" Nicholas said.

"He's trying to cripple the will of the Patriots to go on with the revolution," Papa said.

Clayton nodded his powdered head ruefully. "That is about the only thing that is holding the Patriots together right now—will."

"They say he's headed for Richmond," Papa went on.

"But most of the plantations of Williamsburg families are on the banks of the James, which leaves them open to plunder by the British army as they make their way there. I hear his men are burning tobacco, just so the Patriots can't export it to France and Spain to buy military supplies. Most of those still living on the plantations have fled here to town."

Oh, Thomas thought. *That's what Betsy Taylor was talking about.* He frowned into his stew. *That must be where those three boys came from.*

"Is Governor Jefferson ready for Arnold in Richmond?" Dr. Quincy asked.

Papa snorted. "All he has is a pitiful militia. You know he has embarrassed Virginia by refusing to prepare the colony for this war. And most of the good fighting men have now gone on to Carolina, leaving us all unprotected."

"What about here?" Clayton said. "I've come here for protection. Will I get it, Father?"

Papa carefully broke his bread over his stew before he answered. "Thomas Nelson has said he'll get the Williamsburg militia ready. They're to take up positions to the south and west of the city. We'll have to defend Jamestown Road, or Williamsburg itself will be taken by the British."

Thomas could hear his heart thundering in his ears. *Williamsburg taken? What does that mean? That we'll be dragged from the town by our hair?*

Perhaps by Alexander?

"I'm sorry to have spoiled your festive supper, my dear," Papa said. He looked down the table at his pretty, round-faced wife. The gray eyes that looked back at him were dewy with tears. "But perhaps I can save it," John Hutchinson went on. He reached inside his deep-blue brocade vest and pulled out a dog-eared piece of paper. "I have here a letter from your son."

"Sam!" Thomas blurted out, knocking over his cider tankard. Fortunately, it was empty, but Clayton still clicked his tongue as he set it upright. Clayton had always taken it upon himself to try to turn Thomas into a gentleman like himself and Papa. But it had always been Sam whom Thomas wanted to be like.

"Read it, John!" Mama said.

As Papa unfolded the paper, Thomas closed his eyes and tried to imagine big-shouldered Sam with his blond head bent to it, his tiny, sparkly blue eyes dancing over the words. Papa read:

My dearest family,

I have just learned that the post rider will be by to pick up mail today, so I must hurry to get this written to you. There is so much to tell, but with so little time I can only write of the most important things.

General Washington has appointed Nathanael Greene as the new commander of the American army in the South. I saw him in Charlotte, North Carolina, and I can assure you he is a fine leader. He has a job I don't envy; he must eliminate Cornwallis's army in three states, and he must do it with only 800 men fit for duty and only three days' rations. The military chest is empty, our clothes are in tatters, and morale is low. I will not even tell you how deplorable the conditions are in our campsites.

"Thank heaven for the boy's good judgment in that," Clayton murmured. He reached over and patted Mama's hand, and Thomas noticed that her face was whiter than the creamware dishes. Papa read on:

But the men are sturdy by nature, most of us having been brought up on farms and plantations, and General Greene has excellent commanders under him. He has brought in Colonel Henry Lee with his legion of some 300 men, and they are finely equipped and well trained—from Virginia, no less. I am at last proud to be a Virginian! Henry Lee's legion is being sent on a secret mission I cannot tell you about, but I can tell you that Nathanael Greene has had the good sense to split up his small army and send them in two different directions in the hope that Cornwallis will also divide his band of 4,000. . . .

"Four thousand to our 800!" Clayton interrupted. "That is a death trap!"

Thomas glared at him. It wouldn't be a death trap with Sam there. He was brave and strong. He could take on five men at a time any day, Thomas was sure.

I had the good fortune to be with the troops who went west. We were warned that we would meet

*Cornwallis at a place called the Cowpens, and we
were ready for him. God was with us, my dear family,
for we were victorious.*

*It is the first battle we've won in months, and it is
glorious. Of course, Cornwallis is in a rage, and he
pursues us relentlessly toward the Dan River, burning
wagons and supplies and other equipment wherever
he finds them. But there is more victory in store for
us, I can tell you, with Greene in command. I am
proud to serve under him, even in the rain and sleet
and snow.*

*I pray that all of you are proud as well. It means a
great deal to me to have your love and blessings.*

Yours,
Samuel Hutchinson

As Papa folded the letter and returned it to his vest, there
was silence at the table except for Mama's quiet crying.
Thomas looked around at the faces. Clayton seemed to be
working hard not to cry himself, and Papa studied his
hands as if the answers to his unspoken questions lay in
the folds of his fingers. But it was Nicholas's face that surprised him most. The gentle doctor looked as if he wanted
to shove back his chair and shout angry words at anyone
who would listen.

"I want no part in war," he had told Thomas.

He must really mean that, Thomas thought.

"I am proud of Samuel," Papa said, "as I am of all my sons."
Clayton gave a dry cough. "I'm certain you would be

more proud of me if I were ordained."

Thomas felt himself rolling his eyes. *Here it comes again,* he thought. *Another argument about Clayton wanting to go to England, where all the bishops are, so he can become a minister. Someone is going to end up stomping out of the dining room.*

"That is, after all, what I was trained for at the divinity school," Clayton went on.

Papa answered with The Look—a way he had of knitting his eyebrows together, pressing his mouth into a stern line, and drilling his eyes into whoever was on the other end. Thomas was glad it was Clayton and not him.

"We have been through this until I am weary of it, Clayton," Papa said stiffly. "If the war with England were not enough to keep me from sending you over there, the smallpox surely is. In your physical condition, you could never withstand it. Don't you agree, Dr. Quincy?"

Nicholas nodded and stared down at his porringer as if he wished he could give any other answer.

Clayton's face was by now pinched and white, and so were his knuckles as he clenched his spoon. Thomas hoped he would hold back the words that were probably shoving at his thin lips.

To his relief, Papa changed the subject. With a sigh, he said, "I may not be able to do anything for you right now, Clayton, but perhaps we can help Thomas."

Thomas's head jerked up.

"How is that, John?" Mama asked.

"You know that with so many leaving Williamsburg, our

grammar school has dwindled to nothing and all of the professors have gone off to serve in the war. But with this new rush of people coming into town to live, we have enough boys for a class now. I understand that a Master Wrigley, one of the plantation teachers, has agreed to serve as instructor for as long as we need him. He'll teach the usual Latin and Greek, geography and mathematics, penmanship, of course, and some writing and higher classics."

"Thomas hasn't taken the entrance examination," Clayton said. "He's not yet 12."

That's right, Thomas wanted to shout. *So let's forget about it, shall we?*

"The school believes this is a time for the relaxation of rules. I'm sure Thomas is ready, after all his studies with Alexander." Papa seemed to be warming to the idea. "My grandfather, Josiah Hutchinson, went to the grammar school when it first opened in 1693, and he was followed by my father and then myself. I had always hoped that all three of my boys would attend." He smiled down the table at Mama. "Would that please you, my dear, to have at least one of our sons right where he should be?"

Virginia Hutchinson smiled and nodded.

Ask me! Thomas thought angrily. *I will give you a different answer!*

But no one did, and they all drifted into the parlor for Evening Prayer. Thomas trailed behind, kicking bitterly at the rug so Papa couldn't see him.

Of course if his father said he'd attend the College of William and Mary Grammar School, he would go. As hard as he had worked to gain his father's respect over the last year, it would be stupid to disobey him now.

But I don't want to go! Thomas shouted inside his head. *Why is everyone fighting so hard for freedom? I am never free to do what I want!*

"Are you coming, Thomas?" Clayton said from the dining room door.

"Is there a choice?" he answered.

And as it turned out, Thomas was the one who stormed out of the dining room.

✝ ✦ ✝

Chapter Four

The sun rose on frosted roofs the next morning—Sunday—and Thomas knew it was going to melt the snow before sunset. That was only one of the things that made his face sour when he went out to the kitchen building to help Malcolm haul in wood. On cold days, Esther wanted a huge stack next to the fireplace.

"What's made you such a Gloomy Gus today, Thomas Hutchinson?" she said as he stacked his armload by the hearth. "Soon I'll have to scrape that face off the floor with a spatula."

Thomas didn't answer as he watched her pour a cup of strong tea and put it beside a slab of bread on the table.

"Don't be eyeing this food either," she said. "This is for Malcolm. He works hard and needs his nourishment."

"And I don't?" Thomas said grumpily. "They're sending

me off to the grammar school—starting tomorrow!"

"Poor fellow," Malcolm said, grinning. He slid into his chair and started in on his bread. "They're making you get an education so you can better yourself. The nerve of them!"

"Hush up, Malcolm," Thomas grumbled. He reached for a slice of bread from the cutting board, but Esther waved at his hand with her knife. He watched miserably as she ambled toward the door.

"I'm going to check on Otis," she said. "He's in the barn with the horses, probably frozen half to death."

"Probably hiding from his wife," Thomas muttered as she closed the kitchen door behind her.

Malcolm chewed thoughtfully. "School isn't all that's bothering you, lad, I can tell. Is it that news you got from your brother Sam last night?"

"How did you know about that?"

Malcolm nodded toward the door with a twinkle in his black eyes.

"Esther? She hears everything!" Thomas said.

"And then she tells me. But she didn't have the details straight about the battle at the Cowpens. You'll have to tell me about those later, eh?"

Thomas nodded glumly. "Caroline is mad at me."

Malcolm cocked an eyebrow. "What is it this time?"

"Her family got a letter, too—from Alexander. He is telling them he's fighting for the British, and she believes that!"

"Why shouldn't she?"

"Because it isn't true! I know Alexander. He wouldn't lie to me!"

"But he would lie to his parents?"

Thomas nodded stubbornly.

"And of course you had the good sense to say all of this to Caroline," Malcolm said dryly.

Thomas nodded again.

"No wonder she's mad at you! How would you like it if she said Sam would never lie to her, but he wouldn't think twice about lying to you?"

Thomas didn't answer.

"Well, you'd better get used to it," Malcolm said. "What with Benedict Arnold coming up the river and Nathanael Greene heading for Virginia with Cornwallis behind him, there is going to be more and more of a difference between Loyalist and Patriot."

Thomas bristled. "Caroline and I don't care about that! We're going to be friends no matter what!"

"We'll see."

Thomas glared and stuffed a hunk of Malcolm's bread into his mouth.

Thomas was already sitting in the Hutchinsons' pew at the Bruton Parish Church later that morning when the Taylors took their places across the aisle. Thomas had managed to sit on the end so he could look over at Caroline during the sermon and give her messages with his eyes. It meant he had to sit next to Clayton, who glared at him every time his feet scraped the stone floor or he lost his place in the *Book of Common Prayer,* but it was worth it if it meant being reassured that Caroline wasn't mad at him anymore.

She was wearing her red capuchin, and when she threw back her hood, Thomas saw that she had a smaller bandage on her forehead this morning. Nicholas must have been by the Taylors' house early, before he went to his Quaker meeting. Thomas craned his neck to catch her eye, but she didn't look over. He only got a jab in the ribs from Clayton's elbow.

The service started then, and all through it, Thomas kept glancing over, knowing any minute she would glance back.

But Caroline kept her brown eyes riveted to whatever she was supposed to be doing and never once looked his way. By the time the service was over, Thomas was crawling out of his skin. He wriggled away from Clayton's watchful gaze and tore outside to meet Malcolm and Patsy and wait for Caroline as they always did. Being servants, the Donaldsons sat upstairs in the gallery.

"She didn't even look at you, did she?" Malcolm whispered to him as they watched the people file out past Reverend Pendleton at the front door.

"Who?" Thomas asked innocently.

Malcolm snorted.

"There's Caroline!" Patsy said.

Braids flying, she dashed toward the Taylors, who were just then emerging from the church. She flew into Caroline's arms and, talking excitedly, pointed toward the boys. Caroline's eyes flickered over them for a second, and then she leaned down to whisper something in Patsy's ear. Uncertainly, Patsy waved at her brother and turned away with Caroline. Neither of them looked back.

"What did I tell you, Thomas?" Malcolm said.

"Shut it, Malcolm," Thomas said.

He was still standing there, breathing like an angry bull, long after Malcolm sauntered off toward the Hutchinsons' house to do his afternoon chores. He jumped when Papa put a hand on his shoulder.

"A person could drive a carriage up those nostrils of yours," he said. "At whom are you about to charge, son?"

Thomas gnawed on the inside of his mouth.

"No one, sir," he said.

Papa gave his shoulder a squeeze. "Your mother has a headache and has gone home. Would you like to join Clayton and me at Wetherburn's for dinner?"

It had been a long time since Thomas had been out to Sunday dinner with his busy father. For the moment, that drove all the hostile thoughts out of his head. A meal at Wetherburn's, especially with so many people now crowded into Williamsburg, was sure to be an event.

The tavern's great room was alive with chattering guests clinking their forks against Henry Wetherburn's fine Chinese porcelain and black slaves in green livery carrying steaming trays of food. Papa led Clayton and Thomas to a table where several men Thomas didn't recognize were already sitting. Thomas stopped dead in his tracks when he saw who sat with them.

It was the three boys from yesterday's snowball fight.

Thomas looked away and gnawed at both sides of his mouth.

"John Hutchinson!" said the man next to the boy with the curled-up lip. "Will you join us?"

When he stood up, Thomas saw that it was Mr. Digges. Thomas had been with Nicholas last summer when he'd doctored the man for a fever. He looked hale and hearty now as he clapped Papa on the back and motioned to the boy.

"You've met my Ulysses, but I'm sure you've never made the acquaintance of my younger son. This is Zachary."

Papa nodded. "A pleasure to meet you, Zachary. You must be about the same age as my son, Thomas."

He put his arm out to pull Thomas in, and their eyes collided. Thomas knew his were smoldering with anger. Zachary yanked his eyes away.

Look at me! Thomas wanted to scream at him. *You don't cut open my friend's head and get away with it!*

Wait until Caroline finds out I had lunch with her attackers, he thought. And then he felt a pang. *If she ever talks to me again.*

Introductions were being made around the rest of the table, and Thomas tried to pay attention. These were names he didn't want to forget.

The boy with the wide face and the watery blue eyes that never seemed to blink was Yancy Byrd. His lower lip hung down as far as Zachary Digges's upper lip curled up. The tall, handsome boy was Kent Fitzhugh. Yancy and Zachary looked warily at Thomas, and he let them know with his eyes that he hadn't forgotten yesterday. But the tallish boy didn't seem cowed at all.

The boys, of course, were all quiet as the men talked and the food arrived. Even with the war pinching off many of his supplies, Henry Wetherburn was still able to cover the table with turkey, veal, chicken, and lamb. There was even a bowl of beans cooked with bacon.

"Well, welcome to Williamsburg, gentlemen!" Papa said. "I'm sorry it had to be under these circumstances, but if there is anything the Hutchinsons can do for you during your stay here, I hope you won't hesitate to call on Clayton or myself—"

"There is one thing you can do, Hutchinson!" Mr. Fitzhugh said.

Papa waited politely, even though Mr. Fitzhugh had cut him off in the middle of a sentence.

"I understand you are something of a peacekeeper in town."

Papa nodded.

"I think now you can keep the peace only by showing that we are prepared to fight. Thomas Nelson is putting together a band of militiamen, is he not?"

"He is indeed, some 400 men," Papa said.

Thomas could see his father's jaw muscles tightening. He didn't like Mr. Fitzhugh's tone.

"I would certainly feel more at ease if you would insist that every able-bodied man over 16 join Nelson and prepare to defend us against Benedict Arnold."

Papa smiled faintly. "Like yourself, sir?"

All three men stiffened, and so did their sons.

"We are men of property who have already contributed our share to the war effort, sir," Mr. Fitzhugh said tightly.

"I am speaking of men who refuse to assist at all."

"Did you have anyone in particular in mind?" Papa said with his teeth close together.

"Those lousy Quakers!"

That came from Mr. Byrd, who slammed a heavy hand down on the table to punctuate his point.

"The Quakers do not believe in war, sir," Papa said in a level voice. "For religious reasons, they are not required to serve."

"And I say that's nonsense!" said Mr. Fitzhugh. "And my friends agree."

Mr. Byrd gave one firm nod.

Mr. Digges looked nervous. "I'm afraid I must, John," he said. "In these troubled times, can we afford to grant anyone that luxury?"

Papa's eyebrows shot up. "Luxury? Is that what you think of religious freedom? My son is eating shoe leather so he can fight—for a luxury?"

"Now, John . . . " Mr. Digges stammered. "My Ulysses will be fighting at his side as soon as he turns 16, but—"

"That is *not* the point," John Hutchinson said.

Thomas grabbed the edges of his chair. Any moment there was going to be an explosion from his father if they kept this up.

"The point is," his father continued, "that I have no business interfering in what a man believes so long as that belief comes from God. That is what this war is all about—the freedom to have those beliefs!"

"Nonsense!" said Fitzhugh. "If the Quakers want that freedom, let them fight for it like the rest of us!"

"You sound like that fool Xavier Wormeley," John Hutchinson said. "I thought when we ran him out of his magistrate's office, I might be done with such foolishness. But now I face it from my fellow planters, educated men who should know better!"

"I fear you are not done with Xavier either, Father," Clayton said. "I hear he has joined the militia himself."

"Then we are in trouble." Papa shook his gold and silver head angrily. He delivered The Look at all three of the men at the table. "You have much more to fear from a fool like Xavier Wormeley serving in the militia than you do from a handful of Quakers who uphold their beliefs and refuse to go to war."

No one seemed to have an answer for that—except Mr. Wetherburn, who sent one of his slaves over to set a tray of desserts on the center of the table. Like true gentlemen, they all cleared their throats and began to talk stiffly of other things.

Thomas took that opportunity to glower at Zachary, Kent, and Yancy. But Zachary glared right back, and Yancy and Kent joined him.

Malcolm and I are going to have to plan a way to get them back for what they did to Caroline, he thought. Once they gave these three fools a run around town, Caroline would know that his friendship was worth more than being right about Alexander. It would only take Malcolm and him a week or so—

"Then our sons will be classmates," Papa was saying in a formal voice.

Thomas's head snapped toward his father.

"That they will," Mr. Fitzhugh said. "And a powerful foursome they will make at the grammar school!"

They're going to school—with me? Thomas thought in a panic.

"Perhaps some good will come of this time in town, then, eh?" said Mr. Digges.

There was a general nodding—except from Thomas. He could only look at the trio and stare in horror.

They were looking at each other with the same horror. But Zachary recovered quickly. He turned his eyes to Thomas and curled his lip.

✠ ⬦ ✠

Chapter Five

It was still dark the next morning when Thomas was helping Malcolm break up the ice in the troughs so Judge, Burgess, and Otis's old horse, Musket, could drink. There was even a pale moon shining down on the frosted Palace Green, where a sleepy militia was gathering for its morning drill.

"School starts at seven o'clock!" Thomas wailed. "And don't tell me how lucky I am to be getting an education, or I'll pop you one!"

"You really frighten me, lad," Malcolm said lazily. He shrugged. "Look at it this way—you don't have to live at the school and wear one of those long, black robes like Sam and Clayton did."

"I don't care," Thomas said sullenly. "I don't want to go."

Malcolm dumped a bucket of oats into the feeding trough.

"I still don't understand why not. You loved studying with Alexander."

"That's different. Alexander didn't shout things and make me recite them back. I know that's what this Master Wrigley is going to do. That's what I've heard most teachers do."

"I wouldn't know," Malcolm said.

Thomas rolled his eyes. "Don't start telling me how you would give your left arm to be in my place. In fact, go in my place if you want to. I'll stay here and feed the horses and—"

"Put up with Esther all day?"

Malcolm's eyes twinkled, and Thomas glowered at him.

"I know what it is," Malcolm said. "You don't want to face those three ruffians who threw the rock at Caroline."

"I'd like to take those bullies," Thomas said sulkily.

"All right, then. There's a good reason to go."

"But I wanted us to have time to plan how to do it, and now they're going to be right under my nose, and we're not ready."

"Don't count on me anyway, lad," Malcolm said. "There's a war on. I'm not sure I have time for such goin's-on."

Thomas stared. It was only because pride nudged him that he blinked and said, "I don't need your help anyway."

But pride faded and loneliness took its place as Thomas trudged across the Palace Green with the sun barely up. Everything seemed deserted—the houses, the shops, even the catalpa trees along the Green, whose bare limbs waved in the wind. There was only the militia preparing for war at the end of the Green, near the Governor's Palace.

The men puffed out frosty breaths as they marched back and forth, while their leader barked orders. Thomas gave them a backward glance and started to move on, when he saw someone familiar in their midst.

A fat man with a black cape trailing behind his uniform waddled importantly across the parade field toward the commander, Thomas Nelson. The fat man waved a finger that even from Thomas's vantage point looked like a sausage.

Clayton was right, Thomas thought. *Xavier Wormeley has joined the militia.*

Thomas wasn't cheered by the thought of the mean-spirited, former magistrate fancying himself defending the town from the British. He slogged on toward the school.

Thomas had been to the College of William and Mary many times visiting Sam, so it was easy to find his class-room in the Main Building. Still, his hands were clammy, and his mouth felt as if he'd just eaten a piece of Esther's bread—with no milk to wash it down. He stood in the doorway with his heart thundering.

Ever since it had been decided at the supper table just two nights before that he would be attending the grammar school, Thomas had been resentful and miserable and even angry—but now there was no denying it. He was scared, too.

It was one thing to spend the mornings with Alexander, juggling balls in the dining room while they recited math drills, or sprawling in the grass under a maple tree reading Homer to each other. It was another to come to this polished place that smelled of books and ink—this place where his brothers had both answered every question and passed every test.

I'm going to fail, he thought miserably. *And I'm going to do it in front of three boys I hate.*

He took a step backward and backed into something. He turned to face a long, black robe.

"Watch where you are going, young man!" said a voice that came directly through someone's nose. A pair of silver-rimmed spectacles looked down at him, framing eyes enlarged three times their size by the glass.

"A scholar must be mannerly, quiet, and industrious in school," cried the man. "He must *not* be heedless, disrespectful, and rambunctious!"

All Thomas could think of to say was "Yes, sir."

Apparently that was the right answer, because the bespectacled man waved toward the classroom as if he were batting at a fly and said, "Get you to your seat, then, and be quick about it. A scholar is punctual. He is *not* slothful."

Thomas bolted into the room, but once again he stopped. The man with the spectacles nearly ran up the back of his leg.

"Take a *seat!*" he said testily.

But still, Thomas could only stare. He had never been in a classroom in his life, not in a real school. His first lessons as a chubby, lisping little boy had been in Esther's lap in a rocking chair in the sunny nursery out at Hutchinson Homestead. Even when Clayton had come to teach at the plantation last year after he finished at the divinity school here at William and Mary, he and the servant children had met in a schoolroom in the house with paintings of Thomas's grandfathers looking down at them. He had never seen anything like this.

The room was paneled in somber wood and had only one tall, narrow window looking out over the college yard. There was a stark-looking desk at the front, and facing it were two rows of three desks each that looked even more straight-backed than the uncomfortable pews at Bruton Parish Church. The classroom looked as unfriendly as a jail cell.

But that wasn't the worst of it. The three desks in the righthand row were already occupied—by Yancy Byrd, Kent Fitzhugh, and Zachary Digges. They had witnessed the entire scene in the doorway, and it had obviously pleased them immensely. They were working so hard to hold back their laughter that it looked as if their faces hurt.

Thomas hurried to the last seat in the other row before the man with the overgrown eyes could bark at him again. He plunged into it, knocking the inkwell out of its hole. It bounced forlornly to the back of the room and landed with a thud against the wall. All three boys plastered their hands over their mouths.

"Well, fetch it, young man!" screeched the man at the front. "A scholar is mindful, conscientious, and aware of his surroundings."

Thomas didn't wait to hear what a scholar was not. He dove for the inkwell and deposited it and himself in their proper places. The man marched to the doorway to peer out, and as if they had heard some secret cue, all three of the plantation boys turned to Thomas and stuck out their tongues. He stared at them, frozen-faced.

The man whirled around and every eye was suddenly on him. He put his hands against the small of his back and bore down on them like an angry goose.

"I was told I would have a full classroom of at least six young scholars!" he cried, as if it were their fault that no one else had appeared.

They were smart enough to run away, Thomas thought in agony. *I wish I had.*

Since no one seemed to have an answer to his dilemma, the man sighed impatiently and began to pace back and forth in front of them. He didn't speak for a long time, which gave Thomas a chance to look him over.

He wasn't as tall as Thomas had first thought. The flapping black robe made him appear to be of sky-high stature—that and the enormous wig that teetered on top of his head. Thomas was sure he'd never seen such a hairpiece. None of the Hutchinson men had ever worn wigs, though Clayton often powdered his own hair to be a fashionable gentleman. Even at that, Thomas was certain this "thing" bordered on the ridiculous.

It was pure white and was swept back from his forehead in a high hump that dropped back suddenly at the back of his head, making him look as if he had backed into a wall. The rest hung down into a tail at the nape of his neck—except for the two fat curls on either side of his face that bore a striking resemblance to Xavier Wormeley's fingers. They were so perfectly rolled that it was possible to see straight through them. As Papa would say, a person could have driven a carriage through either of them.

Who is this person? Thomas thought. *It can't be—*

"My name is Louis Wrigley," the man barked suddenly through his nose. *"Master* Wrigley to you. I am your teacher."

He stared them all down as if he were waiting for someone to dispute the fact. Thomas didn't dare breathe.

"Now then," he said, commencing to pace again, "you are under my tutelage for one reason and one reason only—to become true gentlemen: courteous, well-spoken, and educated. You will achieve that by doing exactly as I say. Is that understood?"

Four heads nodded, Thomas's the hardest.

"Let us begin with my rules," Master Wrigley said in his nasal voice. "You will appear for lessons promptly at seven o'clock. If you are absent, you may not return without a note from your father. You are to behave with decency and sobriety on the way to and from school, being careful to never utter any rude or uncivil expression or call your schoolmates by nicknames. You will avoid ranting games and quarreling during leisure time, and you must be quiet and industrious in school. All lessons will be neatly copied in your copybook so they can be studied at home. We will begin reciting three days from today. All recitations will be letter perfect. A scholar is conscientious and studious. He is *not* lazy and careless."

Master Wrigley stopped to take a breath, and Thomas's mind reeled. He'd been right in the beginning—he was going to fail. There was no way under heaven he was ever going to remember all of this.

The teacher inhaled noisily and continued. "You will remember that a scholar is amiable, benevolent, and for-giving. He is not revengeful, arrogant, and—"

As Master Wrigley continued to rant and wear a path in the wood floor, Thomas pictured himself being thrown from the classroom for being revengeful, arrogant, and slothful because he didn't know what any of those things were. And then he imagined standing in the doorway of Papa's library, trying to find the words to tell his father that he had failed. And then he conjured up the image of Papa's Look as he listened.

"—responsible, and truthful." Master Wrigley stopped once more for breath in front of the window and turned to gaze out as if to gather another list of things for Thomas to become.

Thomas felt eyes on him, and he glanced at the other row of desks. The three boys were gaping at him. As soon as his gaze met theirs, all three of them crossed their eyes and stuck out their tongues like a trio of lizards. Thomas gasped.

"We are a country at war!" Master Wrigley cried from the window. He whirled around. Three tongues retreated into mouths. "You cannot expect schoolbooks and paper for such as yourselves! You must rely on my dictation, and you must copy it perfectly if you are to learn. . . ."

And then he was off again, pacing back and forth in front of them in a chicken-like frenzy. This time Thomas only

half listened. He looked again at the row of his schoolmates. Next to him, Zachary Digges stretched out a cau-
tious hand—and pinched Thomas hard on the side of the
leg. Before Thomas could even react, Zachary had pulled
his fingers away and folded them on his desk in a gentle-
manly fashion.

Anger burned up Thomas's backbone like a rope on fire.
His eyes bored into the side of Zachary's head, willing him
to look at him. As soon as Master Wrigley turned his back
to the classroom again, Zachary glanced his way. So did
Yancy and Kent. And all three of them poked their fingers
up their noses.

Seething, Thomas clenched his fist and poked it toward
Zachary. In that instant, the threesome turned their faces
away—and Master Wrigley whirled around.

"What are you about there?" the teacher cried. "You, the
big clumsy oaf! Come here at once!" And his swollen,
bulbous eyes fell squarely on Thomas.

☥ ☥ ☥

Chapter Six

"What do you mean by threatening your school-mate?" Master Wrigley demanded.

With a wrench of Thomas's arm, he pulled him out of his desk and dragged him to the front of the room.

"Answer me!" the man cried.

"I was merely—"

"You were doing nothing of the kind! You are guilty of misconduct, and you will be humbled before your fellows! Do you hear?"

Thomas would have had to have been deaf not to. Master Wrigley had pulled him so close to his face that Thomas could see the veins in his magnified eyes as if they were roads on a map.

"I need only one culprit to make an example of," the

schoolmaster said, his voice squeezing through his nostrils. "So let this be a lesson to the rest of you!"

Thomas looked out at the rest of them and wished he hadn't. Kent could barely stay in his seat, he was so excited, and Yancy's spongy face was a delighted red all the way out to the tops of his ears. But it was Zachary who seemed to be enjoying himself the most. A person could have driven two carriages through the open-mouthed smile he was trying to hide from Master Wrigley.

It would have been enough to make Thomas yank his arm away from the schoolteacher's rigid grasp if Master Wrigley hadn't chosen that moment to produce the final insult. Still holding on to Thomas's sleeve, he reached behind his desk and pulled out a stool. Thomas stared at it.

It had only one leg.

"You've never seen a unipod before, I see," Master Wrigley said. He gave his lips a satisfied smack. "We teachers call this a dunce stool. You will spend no less than 10 minutes on this—10 minutes without falling, that is. And you will do it wearing this."

Once more he reached behind the desk and brought out a tall, pointed cap with a sign dangling from it.

"BABY GOOD-FOR-NOTHING," it said.

The cap was plunked on Thomas's head, and he was shoved onto the stool. It fell over at once—and the teacher was the first to laugh.

"Bumbling boy!" Master Wrigley shrieked. "You thought to strike another student, and you cannot even sit upright on your stool!"

His laughter, which also seemed to ooze from his nose, gave the boys permission to giggle, too. And they did— long and loud.

Thomas felt himself burning all the way to his toes as he got up from the floor and struggled to keep the one-legged stool upright. It was only by staring them all down that he was able to keep from hurling the wretched piece of furniture at them and tearing from the room.

I will sit upright on this! he told himself fiercely. *And I will not fall down. And when I leave here I will never come back again. I will tell Papa I'll work with Francis 20 hours every day, but I won't come back here!*

After five tries, Thomas was finally able to keep his balance, and he sat on the wobbly stool for 10 minutes. With every second, the cap with its sign burned hotter on his head, until he thought his hair would singe. But he didn't flinch. He only thought of leaving and never, ever coming back.

For a while Master Wrigley led the laughter. When it seemed that it was no longer interesting to him, he began to drone on about conjugating Latin verbs and making Q's properly, while the boys continued to stare at Thomas and smirk at him with their eyes. Finally, the schoolmaster pulled his watch from his pocket and gave a disappointed sigh.

"I suppose your time is over, young man," he said. "Take your seat, and see that you never threaten another student as long as you shall live."

It was all Thomas could do to go down the aisle—and not out the door.

The morning wore on like a sermon that wouldn't end. There was a recess for dinner at eleven o'clock, and Thomas strode sedately through the knot of three to get to the door. He was going straight to his father and then to Francis's shop to work.

That's where I belong anyway, he thought. *I know what to do there.*

But at home, his father's library door was shut tight, and neither Papa nor Clayton came out for dinner. Even Mama was away from the house, collecting old clothes from some of the townswomen to make bandages for the hospital. Thomas took his dinner in the kitchen building, where Esther was making a foul-smelling soup. Otis and Malcolm, she said, had taken the grain Clayton had brought from the plantation to the mill.

"You survived your first mornin' at the fancy school," she said. "And after all that whinin' about not wantin' to go."

Thomas grunted and splashed his spoon in his soup.

"Don't be a-dawdlin'," she said. "You don't want to be late gettin' back."

"I'm not going back."

"Well, it's certain you are!" Esther said without the slightest hesitation. She looked at him narrowly from under her cap. "Have you gone and got yourself into some kind of trouble already, Thomas? I'd thought you done some growin' up of late, but that temper of yours—"

Thomas scraped his chair back and stood up.

"There's the boy," she said, clucking her tongue. "You go and get your lessons now."

Tonight I'll tell Papa, he promised himself as he trudged across the Palace Green. *And after school, I'll go to Francis and tell him I'll be working for him all day now, instead of just in the afternoons.*

Now if he could only control that temper of his for the next few hours. *I'll just pretend to be doing my lessons,* he decided, *and I'll keep away from those scoundrels.*

It was a quiet afternoon in the classroom. Master Wrigley finished telling them how difficult their work was going to be and set about proving it. For Thomas, between scribbling down the list of Latin nouns the teacher gave them to memorize and writing their multiplication tables 50 times, there was barely time to take a breath. The boys never looked at him, and as the afternoon wore on, Thomas felt more lighthearted. Just a little while longer and it would be over.

At five o'clock when Master Wrigley dismissed them, the three other boys shot off as if they had been released from jail. Thomas flexed his aching fingers and followed more slowly.

"Well, sir," Master Wrigley said from his desk. "I trust you learned your lesson today."

Thomas stopped stiffly in the doorway, but he didn't turn around. "Yes, sir," he mumbled.

"I will thank you to look at me when you address me, young man!" the teacher cried. "Or you will find yourself atop that stool again!"

Anger singed up Thomas's backbone, and he slowly turned to look at the man in the ridiculous wig.

"Well?" said Wrigley.

"Sir?"

"What have you to say for yourself?"

"Nothing, sir," Thomas said.

For a moment it looked as if Master Wrigley were going to go for the stool and make Thomas sit on it all night. But then he sniffed and returned to scratching his quill pen across a page. "We shall see about that," he said. "Run along now."

Thomas did—all the way down the Duke of Gloucester Street.

Stupid, horrible man! he thought as he ran. *I'm just glad I never have to go back there!*

Darkness was already falling over Williamsburg, leaving the streets looking as cold and deserted as they had been that morning. Most of the shops were already closed, and Thomas's heart sank when he reached the apothecary and found old Francis preparing to close up for the day.

"I'm sorry I'm late, sir!" Thomas said as he hurried up the steps and into the shop.

Francis Pickering peered at him over his spectacles and shook his balding head. "I wasn't even expecting you. Your father came by and told me he'd enrolled you in the grammar school." Francis walked over and closed the door behind him. "It's time you continued your education," he said as he tottered on his stiff old chicken legs toward the counter to blow out the candle. "You're too bright to be nothing more than an apothecary's apprentice."

Thomas stood in the middle of the shop whose very

smells and creaks and jars he loved, and he blinked. "But that's what I want to be. And besides, I don't think I'll be going back to that school—"

"Now you see here, boy," Francis cut in. "You will go to that school and get your education. I can get along fine without you here. Heaven knows you're always underfoot and breaking my jars anyway. Now don't be a fool, and get on with your studies."

"But—"

"Enough now. Get along home. I can't afford to be burnin' candles for mindless conversations."

Thomas stared as Francis skittered like an old bird to the coat hook and pulled down his jacket. Hurt, angry tears burned at the backs of Thomas's eyes.

"Your time here is done, Hutchinson," Francis said as he poked his gnarled old arms into the sleeves. "You get on with the important things now."

On the way home, Thomas felt as empty as the cold, naked streets he passed through. All this time, he'd thought Francis needed him in the shop—and Nicholas, too. He read the tiny print on the labels for Francis when the old man's failing eyes were too tired to see them. He kept Nicholas company on the long rides back from doctoring patients on the outskirts of town. He knew what to do for hurt or sick people until Nicholas or Francis could get there with medicine.

All day he'd thought to tell Papa he was needed more at the apothecary than at that wretched school where he was tormented and humiliated. But maybe that wasn't true. Francis had said it himself: He was always underfoot, always breaking things.

Maybe I'm just a "bumbling boy" after all, just like that Master Wrigley person said I was, Thomas thought. He knocked the muddy slush from his boots at the back door of the Hutchinson house. And maybe now there was no way to convince Papa that he shouldn't go back to school.

He was about to climb the stairs to his room when Mama appeared on the landing above, smiling down at him.

"There's our scholar!" she said. "Your father and Clayton are expecting you in the library. They're anxious to hear how your day was."

Thomas gnawed at his lip. *And what will I tell them?* he thought. *That I've already gotten in trouble? That I'll never pass, and there's nothing else for me to do because Francis doesn't need me anymore?*

"I'll go in later," Thomas said and continued up the stairs.

"Your father wanted to see you as soon as you arrived—" Mama started to say.

But down the back hall a door opened, and Clayton stuck his well-combed head out. "It is Thomas, Father," he said over his shoulder. To Thomas he said, "Father will see you now."

There was no escaping it. Thomas turned and headed to the library. Not even the smells that always wafted from that room—the leather and the licorice—could comfort him. He stood before the desk and said, "Yes, sir?"

Papa looked up from his papers, his heavy dust-colored eyebrows tangled together in a questioning knot. "What is this?"

"What is what, sir?"

"This face dragging on my rug." Papa motioned with his quill pen toward a chair. Thomas sank into it like a stone.

"You look as if you've spent the day in the stocks and pillory," Papa said.

I did, Thomas wanted to say. But he shook his head politely. "No, sir," he said.

Papa examined Thomas with his piercing gaze. "This Master Wrigley, I know nothing of him. He's much different from your Master Alexander, I presume."

That's when the tears started climbing up the back of Thomas's throat. He swallowed hard to keep them back. "He is," he said in a thick voice.

"I'm certain you'll grow accustomed to that in time," said Papa. "We cannot expect every teacher to be as gifted as young Taylor."

Thomas couldn't answer this time. He only shook his head.

Papa was still watching him closely. "And what of the other boys in your class? Digges and the others? I trust you'll become fast friends with them. A boy's schoolmates become his lifelong friends, and you have not had that opportunity until now."

Thomas couldn't just swallow that one. He felt himself going stiff in the chair, and he gripped the arms to keep from flying across the desk and screaming, *I hate them!*

I hate them all! The anger that had gone cold after he'd talked to Francis began to simmer again.

"Did you join them for games after school?" Papa asked. "Is that why you were late in coming home?"

Thomas shook his head.

"Pardon?" Papa said. His eyes were boring so deeply into Thomas's face that he could almost feel them drilling. "I don't believe I heard you."

Thomas squirmed miserably. "I don't think I'll be playing many games with those boys, Papa," he mumbled.

"Thomas," Clayton said sharply.

Thomas looked to where his brother stood leaning against the bookcases.

"Have you already begun to torment the other students? I remember how you treated the servant children in our class at the plantation. I thought you'd learned to—"

That was it. That was all Thomas could take. Whether he had a place at the apothecary shop or anywhere else in the world, he wasn't going to go back to that school where he was the one to be blamed for everything.

"That school is a wretched place!" he cried as he bolted from the chair. "I won't go back!"

John Hutchinson stabbed his pen into his inkwell and scraped back his own chair. The Look was etched firmly in his face as he stood up.

"Perhaps we should begin this conversation again," Papa said, leaning his weight on his hands. "I thought I just heard you tell me what you are *not* going to do. I'm sure I was mistaken."

Clayton cleared his throat importantly. "All the Hutchinson men have attended the College of William and Mary. I would hardly call it a 'wretched school.'"

Thomas turned on him. "It did you a lot of good to go there, didn't it—brother?" he shouted at him. "You can't even be ordained!"

There was an explosion from the direction of Papa's desk. "Leave this room at once, Thomas Hutchinson! At once, I say!"

And Thomas did, taking the steps to his own room two at a time—steps he couldn't see through his blinding tears.

✠ ✠ ✠

Chapter Seven

hat's it, then, Thomas thought as he threw himself across his feather bed and buried his head in the down. Life as he had come to know it was now over.

Alexander, Sam, Francis, Nicholas, Caroline—they were all gone and their places had been taken by miserable wretches like Yancy, Kent, and Zachary—and Master Wrigley. There was no one left to go to for anything. Now even his father had sent him away in shame.

Thomas was about to tear into his quilt with his fists when he stopped suddenly and rolled over.

Don't make the same mistake you made last fall, his thoughts seemed to say. *There is Someone else.*

"God?" he said out loud to his ceiling. "I'm here. Are you?"

And, of course, He was. Thomas could feel his chest

calming down and his fists coming out of their white-knuckled balls. He got up on his knees in the middle of the bed.

If there's one thing I've learned since I've come to Williamsburg, he prayed, *it's that I can't do it all by myself. Please, God, help me.*

It always seemed that once he got started talking to God, the words just didn't stop.

Please, Lord, don't let Alexander be a Loyalist anymore, but please let that be all right with Caroline, because she's my best friend and I hate it when she's angry with me. And, God, please let the war be over soon so it won't matter anyway and Sam will be home safe and there won't be any more fighting at the dining room table. Please let Clayton be ordained, and that will really put an end to all the arguments. And most of all—and this is the one I hope You will answer first, Lord—will You please take me out of that school? Please, maybe let something happen to Master Wrigley—not something bad like he gets the fever and dies—just something that will take him away from there, and those three worms with him. And God, please, when I don't have to go to that school anymore, please make Francis and Nicholas want me back at the apothecary. That's all I ask, Father. In the name of Your Son, our Savior Jesus Christ. Amen.

The prayers in the *Book of Common Prayer* that they used in church always ended that way. With them said, Thomas felt as if he'd done everything right, and it was all in place.

He only hoped God answered some of them before Papa sent for him.

But Papa didn't send for him. Even though Thomas stayed in his room all through supper—and ate the bread Malcolm sneaked up to him, telling him he wouldn't have wanted any of Esther's nasty soup anyway—no one pounded on his door and told him to report to his father in the library.

Thomas fell asleep early, and something woke him before dawn. He drifted in and out of sleep after that, wondering what it was. When he went downstairs to help with the wood, Malcolm told him it had probably been his father leaving for Richmond.

"Richmond!" Thomas said. "Isn't that where Benedict Arnold is headed?"

"That it is, lad," Malcolm said. "Your father will be right in the thick of it."

Thomas bit at his mouth to keep the hurt off his face. *Papa didn't even say good-bye,* he thought. *He must really be angry with me.*

"I wouldn't worry about it, lad," Malcolm said as he hoisted two pieces of wood up on his shoulder. "John Hutchinson can take care of himself."

"Who said I was worried?" Thomas said. And then he added to his long list for God: *Please let Papa forget that he's mad at me before he comes home, and please make sure he comes home.*

As Thomas made his way through the bleakness of gray and brown toward the college later that morning, he wondered when his other prayer—about taking him out of school—would be answered. *Maybe Master Wrigley was called away in the night, too—to rescue relatives living in Richmond.*

He was considering the fact that the pinch-nosed teacher didn't look as if he could rescue so much as a cat from a tree when he heard someone calling from across the school yard.

"Hutchinson! You are young Hutchinson, aren't you?"

Thomas stopped and watched as a tallish boy of about Sam's age hurried toward him. When he got closer, and Thomas could see the thorny eyebrows that nearly met above his eyes, he realized it was Ulysses Digges. He and Sam had been good friends.

But Thomas tightened as he drew near. This was Zachary Digges's brother. Maybe this meant trouble.

"You *are* Sam Hutchinson's brother, aren't you?" Ulysses asked when he reached Thomas's side.

Thomas started walking and nodded. Ulysses hugged his books to his chest and squinted at the cold.

"I was wondering," he said, "have you had any word from Sam?"

"Yes," Thomas said woodenly.

"Well?"

Thomas hunched his shoulders. "He's off fighting."

"I know," Ulysses said. To Thomas's surprise, his voice was filled with awe. "I didn't have the courage he had to

run away and fight for what he believes in. I wish I could
be more like him. We all do."

Thomas couldn't help the pride that swelled up in his
chest—and pushed some of the anger aside for the moment.

"He's in North Carolina now," Thomas said. "Being
chased toward Virginia by Cornwallis. He was at the Cowpens, you know."

Ulysses looked impressed. "The Cowpens? What's that?"

"Only the first American victory in . . . well, in months!"
Thomas said.

"And Sam was there?" Ulysses cried.

"That's right," Thomas said. More words crowded to get
out. "He's going to help win this war. We're going to have
our independence because of men like Sam."

Ulysses nodded. "I'm going to tell the others."

It's as if Sam were a hero, he thought as he watched
Ulysses hurry away. *He disobeyed Papa's orders and made
Mama cry—and even me a little bit. But Ulysses said he
had the courage to fight for what he believes in.*

Thomas bent his head as he walked on through the cold
toward the Main Building, and he prayed as he walked.
God, will you give me that courage, too?

Master Wrigley was there when he reached the classroom, adjusting his wig in the reflection of the window.
And Yancy, Kent, and Zachary showed up, too, all with con-
tempt for Thomas in their eyes. But things looked a little
different in Thomas's mind than they had yesterday.
Thomas took his seat thinking, *You won't look that way
for long. God is going to be my helper.*

He felt braver already.

But even though the Terrible Trio made no attempts to rile Thomas, something else happened that popped his fragile little bubble.

While Master Wrigley was squeezing Latin verbs out through his nose, Thomas felt the boredom that comes with already knowing everything that's being talked about. Papa had been right—Alexander was a gifted teacher. None of what Master Wrigley was whining about was news to him. His fears about failing his lessons were fading fast.

When the teacher went to his desk at one point to consult the book lying open there, Thomas sneaked a look out the window in hopes of finding something interesting to look at. He'd never had to do that with Alexander, but it had been a common occurrence when he was in Clayton's class at the plantation. Clayton had often accused him of looking out to see if there were any frogs flying by.

But it wasn't airborne frogs that caught Thomas's eye as his gaze wandered out over the college yard. It was two girls, one in a red capuchin leading a smaller girl in a chase from one patch of snow to another.

It was Caroline and Patsy playing together. Thomas couldn't take his eyes from them as they cavorted, throwing their heads back and grinning, one a slice-of-melon smile, the other a charming, crooked-toothed grin. Sadness swept over him, and he longed to be out there with them.

Only they won't even talk to me now, he thought unhappily. That was going to change, surely, because he'd talked to God. But He sometimes took so long.

"If you haven't enough to do, young man," whined a voice above him, "I can certainly arrange for another bout with the unipod. That would provide us all with entertainment, eh?"

Master Wrigley nodded at the other boys until his wig wobbled. They all nodded back as if they were scandalized by Thomas's behavior.

"Sorry, sir," Thomas said between his teeth.

"You will be if I find you have not been paying attention! Conjugate the verb *amo* in the present tense as I have just done."

"*Amo, amas, amat, amamos, amatis, amant,*" Thomas chanted automatically. He and Alexander had made a song out of it last summer to be sure he would never forget it.

Master Wrigley looked stunned. "See that you continue to pay attention, then," he said abruptly and marched back to his desk. "There will be a recitation tomorrow."

Thomas let his eyes wander to the next row. Zachary Digges was sliding his teeth over his thumbnail and observing him. He gave Thomas a warning look and turned away.

Thomas spent the evening in the parlor with Mama and Clayton so the family had to have only one fire going. Clayton read, Mama sewed, and Thomas glared at his copybook.

Once or twice Clayton looked over the top of his book as if he were about to say something. But when Thomas caught his eye, he went back to his words with a sniff.

He isn't speaking to me either, Thomas thought. And maybe that was just as well. He went back to the irregular verbs he could already recite backward and forward and gave a sniff of his own. He hoped his prayers were answered soon.

There was a knock on the parlor door then, and Malcolm put his head in. His nose was red from the cold, and he was out of breath. Thomas knew from the familiar bright look in his eyes that he had news.

"Pardon me, Mistress Hutchinson," Malcolm huffed, "but I thought you'd want to hear what the town crier just passed down the Duke of Gloucester Street with."

Clayton was on his feet. "Is it Richmond?"

"Yes, sir. Benedict Arnold has set fire to the city."

"But John is there!" Mama cried, as if that alone kept it from being possible.

"Anything else?" Clayton said to Malcolm.

"No. The crier put his two bits in, of course, sayin' that looks like certain defeat for the Patriots. But I don't believe it. Not for a minute!"

Clayton nodded absently and waved him away. Mama was crying softly into her hands.

"You must be brave, Mother," Clayton said to her as Malcolm shot him a dark look and left the room. "Father will be safe. He's in God's hands."

"Do you think so?"

"I know it!" Clayton said, as if he were scolding her. "And so should you. You must have faith."

Mama nodded and cried some more. Thomas took that opportunity to slip out the door himself and run for the kitchen building. Surely Malcolm knew more.

As he approached the kitchen, Thomas glanced through

the window to see if Malcolm were there. The picture framed by the windowpanes made him skid to a stop.

Caroline was there, talking earnestly to Malcolm from the circle of her red hood. Thomas's thoughts shouted over each other to be heard. The loudest one froze him in place.

She's on their side! it cried. *The people who are trying to burn Papa in Richmond.*

She's the enemy now.

✝ ✦ ✝

ike a boy made of ice, Thomas finally opened the door and went into the kitchen building. He didn't look at Caroline as he hurried to the fire as if he were going to warm his toes.

"Thomas, lad!" Malcolm said. "I was hopin' you'd be comin' out here. Your brother Clayton hasn't much time for 'servants.' I had to take my leave, you understand. But I wanted to tell you—"

"Do you know more about Richmond?" Thomas cut in. He still couldn't look at Caroline, not until he figured this out.

"I was just tellin' the lassie here that Governor Jefferson packed up his government and left for Charlottesville before the British arrived. Your papa's probably tryin' to calm the people he left behind."

"You think he's all right, then?" Thomas asked.

"I know it like I know the back of my hand, lad! John Hutchinson's a wise man. I can't imagine him bein' captured or caught by surprise."

For once, Thomas was glad Malcolm seemed to know everything. Those were just the words he wanted to hear. Letting out a sigh of relief, he chanced glancing at Caroline. She was looking straight at him with her round brown eyes.

"Yes, sir, you should be proud of your father, lad," Malcolm was saying.

"I am." Thomas sank down on the hearth and put his hands out to the fire. He could still feel Caroline watching him.

"You'll be just like him someday," Malcolm went on, "if you get your schoolin' the way he wants you to."

Thomas snorted. Malcolm's dark shaggy eyebrows went up.

"What was that for?" Malcolm asked.

"If you mean by *schoolin'* that wretched grammar school they've planted me in, I'd sooner be like Xavier Wormeley!"

Malcolm unfolded his lanky legs and leaned his forearms on his knees. His black eyes were sparkling. "Well, well, lad," he said. "This is more interestin' news than the burnin' of Richmond! What's happened?"

Thomas only studied Malcolm's face for a moment to be sure it was safe before he opened his mouth and let the whole, horrible story flood out. When he finished by relating

Master Wrigley's announcement that they would have to recite in front of each other tomorrow, Malcolm plucked a straw from the hearth broom and chewed on it thoughtfully.

"So you'll be wantin' to show these bullies, then," he said.

Thomas nodded. "I have to. It looks like I'm going to have to stay there, and I can't do it unless I get them."

"There's only one way to get them, Tom, as far as I can see."

Both boys stared. It was Caroline who had spoken. She had her hands on her tiny hips and her eyes were blazing. Thomas had to will himself to close his mouth, which had dropped open.

"And what would that be, lassie?" Malcolm said. "Are you going to turn Martha loose on them?"

She brushed that question aside impatiently. "You say you already know all the things that Master Wrigley person is teaching."

Thomas nodded, still in a daze.

"All right, then. Show them up tomorrow. Recite circles around the lot of them!"

Malcolm chuckled. "I think she has a point there, lad."

But Thomas scowled. "What good would that do?"

"It would make them mad, sure enough," Malcolm said, "and they'd know they weren't dealing with a numskull."

"Make them look stupid in front of the teacher," Caroline said, "just the way they did to you."

But Thomas wasn't convinced. "What if they know just as much as I do—or more?"

"Three blighters who spend their time stickin' their tongues out at people?" Malcolm said. He hissed through his teeth. "Now *those* are scholars."

"Besides," Caroline said matter-of-factly, "they didn't have my brother for their private tutor."

Alexander. The thought of his teacher moved over Thomas like a cloud. If Alexander hadn't left to do whatever it was he was doing, none of this would be happening. The sadness in him was so heavy that he couldn't move.

"You don't want to try it because you're afraid. Isn't that right?" Caroline said.

Thomas's eyes jerked toward her. "Are you calling me a coward?"

"Maybe."

Thomas folded his arms roughly. "I'm not! I just don't think it will work. You're a girl. You don't know how boys—"

"Fine, then, Tom Hutchinson," she burst out. "Be your stubborn self! Try to fight it out with your fists—like a boy! But don't come running to me with your nose all bloody and say, 'Caroline, I should have listened to you!'"

With that, she gathered her cape around her and flounced out, slamming the kitchen door behind her. As soon as her footsteps had faded across the yard, Malcolm collapsed onto the hearth, roaring.

"What is so funny?" Thomas asked.

"That little slip of a thing tellin' big Thomas Hutchinson just how it is!"

Thomas could feel his scalp going red. "She doesn't know how it is!"

Malcolm finished his guffaw and wiped a tear from the corner of his eye. "I think she does. I would try it if I were you, lad."

He doubled over again, and it was Thomas's turn to storm out of the kitchen. His slam of the door echoed through the yard as he stomped up the back steps and on to his room.

But for all the sureness in his steps, his mind was a jumble. Caroline was surely on the other side, what with the British now threatening his own father. So why was she trying to help him?

It doesn't matter, Thomas thought. *It's a stupid idea, and it isn't going to work anyway.* He sniffed and closed his eyes. *But I'll try it. And You'll help me, won't You, God? You'll help me show up those bullies.*

The next morning, Master Wrigley looked more like he was about to conduct an execution than a recitation. He was dressed in black, and he held a small horsewhip in one hand, which he slapped against the other as he looked around the schoolroom.

Thomas blinked as he watched him. His eyes burned from sitting up with a candle until very late, studying his copybook. He knew all the answers, but there was too much at risk for him to make a mistake.

Please, God, he prayed as Master Wrigley pranced back and forth, building the tension. *Please let me know everything—and show them.*

Caroline most of all, he added.

"You there!" Master Wrigley said shrilly. He snapped the whip toward Yancy Byrd. "You will recite first!"

Thomas gnawed at the inside of his mouth as Yancy struggled to squeeze his wide form out of his desk. If this boy knew all the answers, this wasn't going to work at all.

Master Wrigley made a sharp turn on his heel and pointed his whip to a spot on the floor directly in front of him. "Stand here!" he barked.

Yancy did. Behind him, Kent and Zachary smothered their mouths with their hands, while Thomas stared at them in disbelief. They were laughing at their own friend.

"Now then, boy!" said the teacher. "Recite in Latin the Roman historian Livy's explanation for the study of history. Page one. Paragraph one."

Thomas closed his eyes and there it was—the paragraph as clearly penned as it was in his copybook.

"Begin!" Master Wrigley said, snapping his voice and his whip at the same time.

Yancy Byrd opened his mouth. The whole room seemed to lean forward waiting for something to come out. Nothing did.

"Begin, boy!" Master Wrigley cried again.

Yancy shook his wide head.

"You do not *know?*"

The head shook again until its ears seemed to flap.

Suddenly, Master Wrigley flicked his wrist, and the horsewhip lashed right over Yancy Byrd's head. The spongy boy gave a yelp and cringed.

"Sit down!" the schoolteacher wailed. "You there!"

He pointed his weapon at Kent Fitzhugh, who slunk up to the front of the room with his head hanging nearly to his belly button. There was no more snickering from the row of desks.

Once again, Master Wrigley executed a military turn and pointed Kent to his spot. He asked the same question.

He got the same response.

Mr. Wrigley swung the whip three times over his head before he snapped it just above Kent's shoulder. "You are as ignorant as your schoolmate!" he cried. "Be seated!"

By now Thomas's heart was thundering in his ears as if he had just been threatened with a lash. He almost felt sorry for Kent as he scurried to his desk and cowered there.

"You!" Master Wrigley cried out.

Thomas's eyes whisked to the front of the room. Master Wrigley was pointing his whip straight at him.

"Yes, sir?" Thomas said.

"What do you *think?* Come up here and *recite—if* you can. *Which* I doubt! It seems I have a classroom full of empty-headed *idiots!*"

Thomas felt exactly like one as he made his way slowly to the front of the room. The paragraph spun dizzily in his head.

"Page one! Paragraph one!" Master Wrigley cried.

Thomas groped for the words, but they were just out of his reach.

"Recite!"

I know this! Thomas thought desperately. *But where is it? Why can't I remember it?*

"You don't know this either, do you?"

I do! I know it! God, help me!

"You are an imbecile and a coward!"

"Hoc illud est praecipue in cognitione rerum salubre ac frugiferum!" Thomas blurted out.

The whip stopped inches from his nose. Master Wrigley's already oversized eyes swelled behind his spectacles.

"Omnis te exempli documenta in ilustri posita monumento intueri."

Thomas took a deep breath. *Please, God,* he prayed desperately. *Please let that be right.*

For a moment, there was no way to know. The boys sat like stone sculptures at their desks, and Master Wrigley stood before him looking as if he himself had been whipped.

But slowly the riding crop dropped to his side, and his lips came unstitched from each other. He turned his head, wig teetering dangerously, and looked at the class.

"Well, I have finally found a boy with a brain in his head," he said. "That was a correct answer—letter perfect, in fact. It is the kind of recitation that I would expect of everyone in this room!"

His voice rose to an earsplitting pitch that matched the crack of the whip as he brought it down on Yancy Byrd's desk. The boy lurched back, and his watery blue eyes bulged and threatened to overflow.

"On the next recitation day, every boy in this room will recite just as this young man has done. Is that understood?"

Three heads nodded in stark terror. None of them dared

move his eyes from Master Wrigley, and Thomas watched them with a voice dancing in his head. *"Make them look stupid in front of the teacher,"* it said to him, *"just the way they did to you."*

And from the looks on the faces that cringed before him, he knew he'd done just that.

✝ ✦ ✝

Chapter Nine

When he left the classroom for dinner that noon, Thomas wondered if he should go to Caroline and tell her she was right. Would she even talk to him?

But when he reached the corner of Richmond Road, a rustling in the hedge chased that thought away.

The hedge had no leaves, but it was so thorny and thick with branches that it was impossible to see through. Out from behind it, three faces popped. The one with the curled lip vaulted over it.

"You think you're smart, Hutchinson—just like your father does," Zachary Digges said.

Before Thomas could answer, someone else leaped over the hedge and wrapped himself around his legs and took him down. Thomas tried to scramble forward, and if it had been Kent Fitzhugh alone he'd been struggling with, he could have shaken him off. But three bodies pounced on him and dragged him through an opening in the hedge, away from the curious eyes of Williamsburg.

Yancy Byrd grabbed his arms, and Kent held his legs. Zachary Digges seated himself on Thomas's stomach and curled his lip right over his face.

"You tried to show us up, just like your papa did our fathers that day in Wetherburn's Tavern! You did it just to make us look the fools, didn't you?"

Thomas couldn't answer. He was gasping for air.

"Would you look at that?" Zachary said, losing his upper lip in his nose. "We've got him scared out of his wits already!"

Yancy snorted joyfully, and Kent nodded in admiration as if Zachary had just recited the entire Declaration of Independence. Thomas managed to find his breath.

"Scared?" he said, wriggling under Yancy's spongy grasp. "I'll tell you who was scared!"

Zachary scrunched his thorny eyebrows together. "Who?"

"You!" Thomas cried.

"Ha! When?"

"Today. In the classroom. When Master Wrigley was cracking his whip. Because none of you knew a thing!"

Kent tightened his hold on Thomas's ankles, but Zachary threw his head of thin, brown hair back and laughed harshly.

"Scared?" he said. He looked as if he smelled a basket of rotting eggs. "*Smart* is what we were. We know when to sit there with our mouths shut, eh, boys? What with that whip flailing about!"

Yancy gave the expected snort, and Kent nodded enthu-
siastically. Thomas writhed to get loose, but Zachary bore
down harder.

"At least we didn't show off for the teacher," he snarled
near Thomas's nose. "Not like you did."

"You can't bear it that I showed you for the fools you
are!"

"You're the fool, Hutchinson—if you ever, *ever* do that
again." He gave Thomas's belly a final trounce, and Yancy
and Kent squeezed his arms and legs one last time. Then
they got up and slipped through the hedge to the street.

"Let that be a warning to you," Zachary said. And then he
disappeared.

Thomas lay on the ground until their voices mingled
with those of the townspeople. Anger pumped through him.

You were wrong, Caroline! he thought savagely.

He scrambled up and jumped over the hedge. He wasn't
sure where he would have gone or what he would have
done if he hadn't heard an alarmed clanging from down
the Duke of Gloucester Street. The town crier was running
toward the college, waving his bell over his head. A crowd
of citizens with panicked faces surged behind him.

"What's that you say?" they were calling to him. "You say
it's the British?"

"A small band of Redcoats is headed toward Williamsburg!"
he called back. "Everyone, head for your homes, and lock
your doors! The British are coming!"

Thomas ran for him with his heart roaring in his ears.
"Is it Benedict Arnold?" he cried.

"Get to your home, boy!" the crier shouted at him. "All of you, get to your homes! The British have been sighted! They're coming here!"

The crowd burst apart and scattered in all directions, clutching their children and their baskets to their chests. Thomas was shoved for several yards in the wrong direction before he pulled away and raced for the Hutchinsons' house.

It was happening. After all the talk at the dining room table and all the arguing in Papa's study and all the reading about it by candlelight with Malcolm in the kitchen building—it was happening. The British were coming to Williamsburg.

Thomas's heart seemed to be working its way up his throat by the time he burst in the front door and slammed it behind him. Mama was in the hall with Esther, wringing her hands together like a pair of rags.

"Oh, Thomas, thank the Lord!" she cried. She pulled him to her and held on. "The British—"

"Thomas!" Clayton barked from behind them. "Go to the kitchen and help Malcolm and Esther bring supplies into the house." He limped toward the door. "I must go to the courthouse to see if there is some sort of plan in effect for the town."

"Don't leave us, Clayton, please!" Mama said.

Clayton shook his head. "I have to, Mother."

Thomas saw that Clayton's face was tinged with gray, the way it was when his heart was ready to give him a spell.

He's as frightened as I am, Thomas thought. *This is real!*

"Go and help Malcolm, Thomas!" Clayton said from the doorway. He opened the door, and Thomas could see people darting across the Palace Green and hear them hurling anxious words to each other. Clayton took a deep breath and hobbled out.

Mama put her face in her hands, and for a moment she was silent. "I wish John were here," she said softly into her fingers.

"There, there," Esther said, putting her old arms around Mama's shoulders. She hugged her as if she were a child. "It will be fine, Mistress Virginia. We're all here to help."

But Virginia Hutchinson shook Esther's arms off and wiped at her tears with the backs of her hands. Thomas couldn't help staring.

"I'm tired of being helpless!" Mama said fiercely. "I feel as if we are at the mercy of this war all the time, and I hate it. I truly do!" She tossed her black curls and sniffed. "What can I do to be sure we are safe, Esther?"

"Now, Mistress, don't you be a-frettin'—"

"I will fret if I please, Esther! Now what would you have me do?"

Esther pursed her lips. "I suppose you could close all the blinds and be sure we have plenty of candles, but—"

"Good, then," said Mama. And with a rustle of silk, she disappeared up the stairs, no longer sniffing. Thomas stared after her. That was not the Mama he knew—the Mama who loved to giggle and pour tea, and who acted as if making bandages for the soldiers were some grand game she was allowed to play.

"Don't stand there a-gawkin', child!" Esther said. "There's work to be done!"

Thomas bolted out the back door and headed for the kitchen. Old Otis was coming across the yard with a cart loaded with firewood. Thomas thought he must be taking it into the house so they could keep a fire going without having to go outside and letting the British see them.

In the kitchen building, the table was stacked halfway to the ceiling with loaves of bread and bowls of mush and packages of salted meat. Malcolm stood staring out the end window toward the Green with a half-empty cloth bag in his hand.

"I'm supposed to help you—" Thomas started to say.

But Malcolm gave a loud *"Shhh"* and waved for him to hush. Thomas joined him at the window.

"What are you looking at?" Thomas whispered.

Malcolm pointed out. "They're already here," he whispered back.

Thomas pressed his face close to the glass. Trotting down the Palace Green on a stately black horse was a man in a white wig, scarlet coat, and white doeskin breeches. His pewter buttons shone in the winter sunlight, and with no visor on his high hat, he shielded his eyes with his hand. A large ring twinkled on one finger.

"I read that it takes a British officer three hours a day to polish his belts and medals and powder his hair," Malcolm said.

Thomas was sure he had never seen so much lace and brass on a man. The Virginia militia would look like a troop of beggars next to this.

"Are they going to take us all prisoner, do you think?" Thomas said.

Malcolm grunted. "And what would be the purpose of that, lad? Are they to drag a bunch of women and children into battle?"

"Then why *are* they here?" Thomas said, scowling.

"I'm guessing they want to use the town to build up their supplies. They must be runnin' low on blankets and wagons and meat and such things."

"They're going to buy them here?"

Malcolm cuffed him on the shoulder. "Don't be a fool, lad! They're going to *take* them. That's why I spent the whole mornin' hidin' salt pork in the hay—except what we'll need in the house, of course." He nodded toward the table. "We'd better get to work packin' this up or we'll have Esther down our throats." He chuckled. "She's probably worse than the British."

Thomas picked up a cloth bag and started to stuff it. His hands were shaking. Malcolm acted as if a British invasion happened every day, but Thomas could hear the excitement in his voice.

"I'll wager they're going to take their broken guns to the gunsmith's and make him do their repairs," Malcolm said. "Won't George Fenton be hotter than his forge over that?"

The door flung open just then, but it wasn't Esther who stood there clutching at her cloak and breathing like a blacksmith's bellows. It was Caroline.

Once again, the painful thoughts crowded into Thomas's

head. *Is she the enemy now?* For now he couldn't even think about what had happened in school that day.

"Thomas!" she cried. "You have to do something!"

"I am doing something," he said. "We have to take all this food into the house—"

"No, you have to do something about Francis!"

Her brown eyes were enormous, and she was shivering.

"Come in and close the door!" Malcolm said. He yanked her inside by the hand and slammed the door behind her. Then he set about shoving the curtains closed.

"Francis probably already knows the British are coming," Thomas said to Caroline. *You're the British now, aren't you?* his thoughts added.

"But he *doesn't* know!" Caroline grabbed Thomas by the shirt. "Listen to me! A British officer just came to call on Papa, to get his help, and I heard them talking—"

Malcolm was at her elbow at once. "What did he say, lassie?"

"He told Papa that they're mostly here to get medicines for their wounded soldiers. He wanted to know where the best apothecary and the best doctor were. He said if they don't give up their supplies, they'll have to force them!"

"No, they can't do that!" Thomas cried.

"Did your father tell them—about Francis and Nicholas?" Malcolm asked. His black eyes were pleading with her.

"Of course he didn't!" Thomas said. "Francis and Nicholas saved Patsy's life, and—"

"Don't be a fool, lad!" Malcolm said. "This is war!" He pulled Caroline toward him by both shoulders. "Did your father tell the British officer where to find them?"

Caroline's face crumpled. "Yes!" she said tearfully. "He had to! And you have to go and warn them!"

But she might have saved her breath. Thomas was already out the kitchen door. As he tore toward the apothecary shop, the words slapped his face like the bitter cold he ran through. *She is the enemy now. No! But she is!*

✢ ✢ ✢

Chapter Ten

"**T**homas! Be careful, lad!" Malcolm hissed after him.

But Thomas didn't even have to think about that. As many times as the Fearsome Foursome had sneaked around town, dodging each other and diving into secret hiding places, Thomas knew how to get almost anywhere without being seen. He reached the apothecary shop— heart pounding, breath gasping—almost before Malcolm could get the kitchen door closed.

The blinds were all drawn and the back door locked when Thomas tried the knob. But he knew Francis was in there. He would never leave his herbs and elixirs at a time like this.

Thomas hurried to the window in the examination room and rapped on the glass. "Mr. Pickering, it's Hutchinson!" he whispered hoarsely. "I have news!"

"Back door!" the old man wheezed.

In seconds, he was opening the door just wide enough for Thomas to wriggle in, and he bolted it securely behind him. He turned and pointed a bony finger at Thomas.

"What are you doing out and about, boy?" he said. "Don't you know the British are coming?"

"They've arrived!" Thomas said. "And they're coming to your shop to take all your medicines and supplies for their soldiers!"

"Who told you this?"

The words stuck in Thomas's throat. A shadow fell across the old man's face, and he nodded sadly. "I knew it would come to that someday. Drat this war!"

He looked as if he were going to stand there all day cursing the British and the Loyalists and the Tories. Thomas tugged at his sleeve. "We have to hide things, sir! And we have to hurry!"

Old Francis drew himself up and darted his eyes around the shop. "Where on earth can we put it where they can't find it?"

Thomas's thoughts ran wild. Every second they stood here brought the British closer to the door. *Please, God,* he prayed. *Help!*

Francis was already gathering armfuls of vials and jars, just the way Malcolm and Esther had done with their food earlier. That gave Thomas an idea.

"Malcolm hid our things in the hay in the stable," he said. "Perhaps we could do that."

"I have no stable, boy!"

"But I do! We could stuff things in bags, and I could run them home. Then you could stuff more and have them ready when I come back!"

Francis shook his balding head, which was now red all the way up to the top with anger and fear. "I can't have you running all over town with those Redcoats about."

"They don't want women and children," Thomas said— as if he'd thought of it himself. "Besides, I know how to go so they won't see me."

"I don't know—"

"Sir, we have to hurry!" Thomas said frantically.

He grabbed a bag he'd carried full of medicines many times for Francis and thrust it into his hands.

"You fill this one, and I'll find more in the cellar. Hurry, sir!"

Francis gave him one more long look through his spectacles before he took off like an old skittering bird for the cabinets. "We'll save the most vital things first," he said as Thomas flew off down the cellar steps. "Heartsease, calendula . . ."

It took only a few minutes to fill two bags. Thomas flung them over his back and went for the back door.

"If anyone catches you, give them the bags and run," Francis said as he lifted the bolt. "We can replace them, but—"

"No one will catch me, sir," Thomas said. After a long look up and down the now-deserted road, he slipped out. He was at the corner before he heard the door close behind him.

There seemed to be no one left in Williamsburg, British

or otherwise, as Thomas easily made his way back to the
Hutchinsons' yard. Even his own house looked as if no one
lived there anymore, and it gave him a chill. He wanted to
run inside, just to be sure the officer in the scarlet coat
hadn't stolen his family away—what was left of them.

But there wasn't time. He went straight to the stables
and emptied the two bags of medicines into a pile of straw
that was out of reach of the horses' curious mouths.

"You watch over those things, Burgess," he said to the
gentle bay. And then he slid from the barn and back to the
apothecary shop.

He tapped on the back window, just as he'd arranged
with Francis before he left. But there was no answering
whisper from inside.

Maybe he's in the cellar packing the dried herbs, Thomas
thought.

The only window to the apothecary basement was on the
side, so Thomas got down on his knees and crawled around
the corner. He was passing the door when he heard voices
from inside. Loud voices.

"I'll do nothing of the kind, Xavier Wormeley!" Francis
cried.

Xavier Wormeley!

Thomas scrambled up and peeked in the side window in
time to see the flabby-cheeked former magistrate flapping
the cape that he wore over his blue militia uniform with
its brownish-yellow leather waistcoat.

"You will or you'll be thrown in jail!" Xavier shouted. "I
have the authority. I am with the army now!"

"You're with that ragtag militia that couldn't save us from an invasion of butterflies," Francis said in disgust.

Thomas saw him teeter back behind the counter. He looked as if he were kicking something aside. *He's trying to hide the bag he was packing when Xavier came in,* Thomas decided.

"Why else would the people be running around like a flock of chickens preparing for the wolf?" Francis went on. "Now I'll thank you to be on your way. I have myself to protect."

"You have the American army to protect!" Xavier cried. "Once again, Pickering, I demand that you turn over your medicines to me for our own men before the British take them away for theirs!"

Francis slammed a gnarled old hand down on the counter. "I won't, I say!"

Xavier didn't answer. He just charged across the shop with his fat arms extended in front of him and snatched the front of the old apothecary's shirt with his sausage fingers and shook him.

"No!" Thomas screamed.

He tore around to the front of the shop and threw open the front door, which Xavier hadn't bothered to bolt behind him. In two leaps, he was across the shop, hauling back on Xavier's cape with both hands.

"Stop it!" Thomas shouted. "Stop it, I say!"

Xavier turned to look, and he let go of Francis. The old man staggered backward and gasped. Thomas dropped the cape and scrambled behind the counter, dodging Xavier's greasy grasp as he went.

"Sir, are you all right?" Thomas cried.

"I will be as soon as this bag of wind blows out of my shop!" Francis coughed and wheezed, but he could still shake his finger at Xavier. "Get out! Get out now!"

But Xavier only straightened his cape indignantly and aimed his poke-hole eyes at Francis.

"I came to prepare you. Start packing your goods, Mr. Pickering. My soldiers will be here in less than one-half hour to collect them. Be ready."

I'll pack them, all right! Thomas thought. He felt as if his face were going to explode. *And then I'll take them right to my stables!*

He nudged the old man in the ribs. "I'll get started right away, sir," he said.

He picked up the half-full bag that Francis had kicked aside and looked into the beady little eyes. Francis nodded —and winked.

Thomas hurried to the last full cabinet and began to empty its contents into the bag.

"You'll want to get that other bag ready, too, Hutchinson," Francis said.

He nodded toward a stuffed bag that sat waiting in the hallway. Thomas nodded—and winked back.

Xavier gave a satisfied sniff. "I knew you would see it my way, Pickering," he said. "In spite of your dealings with the Loyalist Taylors, you are a Patriot at heart."

"Then go away and let me be one," Francis said, spitting the words at him.

"In a moment." Xavier cleared his throat as if he were about to make a weighty announcement. "I have one more piece of business with you before I go. You are to deliver this to Dr. Nicholas Quincy."

Thomas stopped packing long enough to watch Xavier produce a piece of parchment and pass it to Francis across the counter. The old man squinted at it.

"What is this, Wormeley?"

"Captain Wormeley, if you don't mind."

"I do mind," Francis said. "The print is so fine on this I can't read it."

"Then let me be so kind," Xavier said. "It gives notice that Dr. Nicholas Quincy is to report to Thomas Nelson, head of the Williamsburg militia, by sundown tonight. He must supply his own blanket and his surgeon's tools—"

"For what?" Francis broke in, his spectacles quivering.

"For duty. The war is here, Mr. Pickering. Our men are going to fight, and some of them are going to be wounded. We have no doctor, at least not until this one reports for duty."

"You can't do that!"

Xavier's head whipped toward Thomas, who stood with an apothecary jar clutched in his hand.

"You have no say in this, boy!" Xavier said. "And this is the army we are dealing with here. There is nothing the almighty John Hutchinson can do about it either." But the "almighty" Xavier Wormeley took a step back. "And do not even consider throwing that jar at me, or you will land in jail next to your sissy doctor friend if he does not do as he is told!" He gave a menacing look. "We beat the bottoms of the feet of such people with a birch cane, you know!"

"He isn't a sissy!"

"Here," Francis said sharply. He held the paper out to Xavier. "If you want Dr. Quincy to have this, you'll have to deliver it to him yourself. I want no part in it."

Xavier snatched the paper and shook his jowls angrily. "Then you are not the Patriot I took you for, Pickering!"

"Thank the Lord," Francis mumbled.

Xavier turned with a whirl of his cape and marched toward the door.

"Keep packing, Hutchinson," Francis said.

"Yes, see that you do," Xavier barked from the doorway. "One-half hour."

When he was gone, Francis fairly ran over to Thomas on his ancient sparrow's legs. "Quickly boy, take these two bags and get home. Tell your father what's happening. I shall try to find Nicholas myself."

"Shall I come back for more medicine?" Thomas asked.

"Never mind that. We must save the doctor from the clutches of that bloated—" Francis stopped himself. "No, it will look too suspicious if I have nothing to give the soldiers when they come, British or American."

Thomas looked down at the full bag that sat at his feet. To look at it, it could have been a bag of laundry, and yet it was so important.

"What's in this bag, sir?" he said.

"I don't know," Francis said. "I can't tell from the outside."

He looked up at Thomas, and a gleam came into his eyes. "I think rags and jars of cinnamon and a few candles might be just the thing for the soldiers, don't you?"

Thomas grinned and nodded.

"Now mark me, Hutchinson," Francis said quickly. "If there are indeed wounded soldiers in the hospital who need my help, I will gladly turn over whatever I have. But in the meantime, my responsibility is to the citizens of this town."

"Yes, sir," Thomas said.

Francis gave him a push with his bony fingers. "You go now. I want your father to know what they're trying to do to Nicholas."

Thomas was halfway home with the two bags of medicine when he realized with a pang that he couldn't tell Papa about Nicholas, because Papa was in Richmond. He started to panic.

God, I know I've asked a lot of You already, he prayed as he ducked behind the well with his yard in sight. *But please, please let Francis find him before Xavier does.*

Thomas didn't want to think about what Nicholas would do when Francis told him. His only choice would be to run away, and then Thomas would be without yet another of the men he looked up to.

"Then I'll be left with only Clayton and Master Wrigley," he mumbled to himself. *Please, God, don't take Nicholas away, too.*

He readjusted the bags on his back and reached down to open the gate. It was wrenched open from the other side, and Thomas was yanked in by a pair of wiry arms.

"I don't know what that is you have in those bags, lad," Malcolm whispered hotly into his ear. "But I have a feeling you'd better hide them quick! The British are comin' right up the Green!"

✠ ⋅✠⋅ ✠

Chapter Eleven

"It's medicine!" Thomas whispered. "We have to hide it in the straw or someone's going to take it from Francis!"

Malcolm shoved him toward the stable.

The horses' building was dank and full of the frosty breathing of the animals, but Thomas felt feverish with fear as he and Malcolm spread the vials and jars on the floor in the corner and dumped most of the hay from poor Musket's stall on top of it.

"You're a smart lad to use my idea!" Malcolm whispered to him as they worked.

"Well, if you're so brilliant, help me figure this one out!" Thomas whispered back. "Xavier Wormeley has an order from the militia to force Nicholas to report to them for duty."

Malcolm wiped out the militia with a toss of his head. "They can't do it. Dr. Quincy is a Quaker."

"I don't think they care about that!"

Malcolm suddenly put his hand over Thomas's mouth and grew stiff. Thomas tried to squirm away until he heard what Malcolm heard. Horses' hooves were approaching, just outside the fence.

"British," Malcolm said almost soundlessly.

The hooves stopped, and voices batted back and forth in low tones. Finally, Thomas heard the crunch of boots on the walk and the creak of the gate opening.

"Here!" Malcolm hissed.

He picked up a currycomb and shoved it into Thomas's hand. Thomas stared at it.

"Brush a horse!" Malcolm whispered.

Thomas came unstuck and dove for Burgess. Malcolm took to combing Musket, who was only groomed about once a year. The old horse whinnied and sidestepped, but Malcolm just whistled at his back.

"So, lad, wasn't that a delicious breakfast Esther fixed for us this morning?" Malcolm said loudly.

Thomas looked at him. Malcolm nodded in desperation.

"Oh . . . yes!" Thomas said. "Those johnnycakes . . . mmmm-mmmm!"

"Hallo there," said a proper voice from the doorway.

Thomas turned to stone, but Malcolm looked up mildly and said, "Hello. Can we be helpin' you?"

Two men in scarlet coats and white doeskin breeches entered the stable and looked around curiously.

"There seems to be no one home in the house," said one of the men.

"Of course not," Malcolm said. "They've all gone to Richmond."

The other soldier snickered. "A stupid move, that."

"That's what I thought, and Thomas here did, too," said Malcolm. "But we're only servants after all, eh, lad?"

Thomas didn't hesitate this time. "That we are," he said. "No one would have listened to us anyway."

"They ordered us to stay and take care of the house," Malcolm went on. "But they'll have no such luck with us. With not a scrap of food left here to eat and no wood to make a fire, we'll either starve or freeze to death." Malcolm gave the currycomb a flourish. "As soon as we've done groomin' these horses, we're off."

The first soldier looked doubtfully at Musket. "You aren't planning to go far, I hope."

"Though *this* is a fine horse," the other soldier said. He put a hand up to stroke Burgess's forelock. "We might do well to take this one, sir."

Thomas opened his mouth to speak, but Malcolm's piercing eyes stopped him. Thomas bit his lip.

"I'd willingly give him to you, too, sir," Malcolm said. "Bein' loyal to the king the way I am."

The first soldier looked at Malcolm suspiciously. Malcolm looked back at him, eyes open wide in innocence. "I'm from Scotland, as you can tell," he said. "Of course I'm a true subject." Malcolm gave them his square smile. "That's why I'm usin' the horse myself—to go and join the British army."

Thomas had to duck behind Musket so they wouldn't see him choking. He heard the second soldier say, "We'll not deprive you then. You know you'll most likely have to trade the beast for a weapon when you join."

"I've heard that," Malcolm said, spreading the Scottish accent thickly through his words. "But I'm willin' to do whatever it takes to get this rebellious band of colonists back into line, eh?"

Thomas peeked over the top of Burgess in time to see the first soldier clap Malcolm on the back.

"You're neither of you old enough, but the army will take you. We need all the good men we can get."

"And this one's a strong one, eh?" the other soldier said, nodding toward Thomas and sizing him up with his eyes.

"He'll serve His Majesty well," Malcolm said.

The two soldiers gave the stable one more going-over with their eyes and moved toward the door.

"Get on your way quickly, then," the first one said. "As soon as we get everything we need, we'll be leaving town. You'll want to be gone before the Patriots take it over again."

"For now, anyway," the other one put in.

They nodded politely and disappeared from the doorway. Thomas held his breath until the hoofbeats faded off down the Green.

"I'm going to lose my breakfast!" Thomas said.

Malcolm grinned and tossed the currycomb away. "All those years thievin' with my father in Scotland made me a good liar—when I have to be," he said. "But I'll tell you, it gave me no pleasure to tell them I was a loyal subject of the king! I'd no more fight for the British than Nicholas would."

"Nicholas!" Thomas cried. "We have to find him!"

"I'll go lookin' for him," Malcolm said. "You go in and tell Master Clayton."

"Why?" Thomas said. "What good can Clayton do?"

"He's seein' after things with your papa gone. He should know."

"All right," Thomas said reluctantly. "But I wish Papa were here."

The sun was starting to set as Thomas ran up the back steps of the abandoned-looking Hutchinson house. The windows stared out blankly without a candle in them, and the back door wouldn't budge when he leaned against it.

He tapped lightly, and it opened at once, as if Otis had been watching him through the crack. Mama, Clayton, and Esther were huddled in the back hall with him.

"My darlin'!" Mama cried. She rushed to him and began feeling his arms.

"I'm not hurt, Mama," Thomas said impatiently. "They only talked to us, and Malcolm told them you'd all gone to Richmond and left us servants here."

Esther put her hands on her ample hips. "What I want to know is, did they take our food?"

Thomas shook his head. "Nor the medicine either. I hid Master Francis's supplies in the straw, too."

"Good, Thomas," Clayton said.

Thomas took a moment to stare at his brother. He wasn't

sure he'd ever heard those two words come out of his mouth together. And then he remembered—

"Clayton," he said, "Mr. Pickering said to tell you what I heard in the apothecary. The militia is ordering Nicholas to serve."

"Oh, dear," Mama said.

Clayton shook his head wearily. "They're throwing effort after foolishness. He'll never do it."

"Xavier Wormeley says if he doesn't, they'll put him in jail!"

"That fat crow!" Esther cried. "Every time he starts a-flappin' his wings, there's trouble."

"There's a law guaranteeing Nicholas the right to abstain from service for religious reasons," Clayton said. "I must go back to the courthouse and see that it's upheld."

He turned and limped toward the front door to fetch his coat from the hook beside it. Mama hurried after him.

"Clayton, you're already exhausted," she said. "Must you go? They'll surely catch you. Isn't there another way?"

As they all followed Clayton to the front door, Thomas saw in the faded light from the parlor window that his older brother's face was ashen and drawn.

"I can't see any," Clayton said. "I must follow God's guidance on this matter."

"Can we help you then, son?" Mama said. There were tears in her eyes. "I can't sit helplessly by anymore!"

Clayton started to shake his head, and then his eyes rested on Thomas. "There is one thing you can do. Thomas, lead the family in prayer. There is power when two or three are gathered together. It will give us all courage."

Then he nodded to them and ducked out into the cold.

For a moment, Thomas was as frozen as if he had followed Clayton out into the bitter afternoon. Mama nudged him.

"We'll gather in Master John's library," she said. "It should still be warm in there. Quickly now."

Suddenly, it seemed to Thomas as if the world had been turned upside down, and everyone in it had fallen into Papa's place. Clayton was going to shake his fist at the courthouse, and Mama was taking charge of the family. And he himself was going to lead prayer.

The family was quickly gathered in the library with the smell of Papa all around them. Mama, Esther, and Otis looked at Thomas expectantly.

Please, God, Thomas prayed with his eyes squeezed shut, *please put the right words in my mouth. I'm supposed to give us all courage.*

He opened his eyes and sighed. So far God had been at his elbow whenever he'd needed to tell Him something. Maybe if he just started talking. . . .

"Father," he said, "please be at Clayton's elbow—and Papa's—and Nicholas's. Please let Francis find Nicholas and help him get away before Xavier Wormeley finds him —and let Clayton get to the courthouse before the British discover him. Protect us here in the house—"

He stopped. He wanted to add, "Please protect Caroline, too," but wasn't she the enemy now? She'd come to them so they could help Francis, but it was her father who had told the British where to find him. No, he wouldn't tell God that part.

"Amen," he said.

"Amen," said a deep voice from the doorway.

"John!" Mama cried.

She flew to Papa, and Esther raised her eyes to the ceiling and said, "Praise the Lord."

"How did you get back from Richmond so fast?" Mama asked. "On angel's wings?"

Papa shook his head wearily and pulled off his greatcoat as if it were an effort. "I never reached Richmond. I received news of the fire before I got there, so I turned around to come home. A small band of British soldiers came into an inn where I had stopped, and I overheard them say they were coming to Williamsburg. I paid the innkeeper's son to ride here and give the news."

"Why didn't you come yourself with the news?" Mama said.

Papa smiled as if it hurt his face. "The British had me somewhat detained in the inn. I got away only after they left."

"John!" Mama cried. "Are you hurt then?"

Esther flapped over to him as if she were going to begin to examine him right then and there. Papa held her off with a tired hand. "I'm only somewhat sore from their searching me. It's nothing a cup of bee balm tea wouldn't cure, eh?"

"We didn't dare light a fire, but we've still some bread and citron water," Esther said.

Papa looked amused as Otis produced both from under Papa's desk.

"We've had to move everything into the house," Mama said. "We were frightened of the British."

"That was wise," Papa said. "Whose idea was that?"

"Clayton's. Now come and sit down, John." She took him by the arm, but he winced and pulled away. His sleeve pulled up with her hand, and Thomas gasped out loud. His father's big arm was black and blue and swollen.

"We may need to call Nicholas if this doesn't improve," Papa said. "But just being back with my family is all I need now." He looked around. "Where is Clayton?"

"A great deal has happened since you've been gone," Mama said grimly. She coaxed him into the chair and told him the news. He was up again the moment she was finished.

"They cannot take Nicholas Quincy!" he said. "That is against a law I fought hard to see voted in!" He looked at Thomas. "That's what you were praying about, then. Thomas, hand me my coat, please."

"John, you can't go! You're barely able to walk!" Mama said.

Papa looked at her. "So is Clayton," he said.

But before Thomas could get his coat to him, Esther bustled back into the room, her hands groping the air.

"Master Clayton is back!" she said. "He can't make it past the parlor!"

They rushed down the hall and found Clayton half on and half off the sofa in the cold room. His face was as white as his linen shirt.

"Good heavens!" Papa cried. He lifted Clayton onto the sofa and put his hand on his son's chest. "It's his heart!

He's having another spell!"

Thomas felt his own heart stop in his chest—and then it exploded into motion again. "I know where there's medicine for him!" he said. "Francis packed the heartsease and calendula first!"

"Get it, then," Papa said. "Quickly."

But Clayton clutched at his father's hand. "I must tell you this first, Father," he said.

Papa leaned in and put his big hand on Clayton's cheek.

"Dr. Quincy," Clayton said. "They've caught him."

"No!" Thomas shouted.

But Papa silenced him with his hand. "Don't worry. I'll go to him and tell him he doesn't have to serve with them." He turned to Clayton. "Where is he now?"

"He told them he would rather rot than have anything to do with war," Clayton said in a voice they could barely hear. "He's in the jail, sir."

✝ ⋅✝⋅ ✝

Chapter Twelve

Thomas had never spent a night like that one.

Malcolm and Francis returned to the house crest-fallen because neither had found Nicholas before Xavier did.

"But tell them your good news, sir," Malcolm whispered to the old man as Francis set to work helping Thomas give Clayton the medicine Thomas had dug out of the straw.

Francis did give a little cackle. "The British got to the shop just before I left to go lookin'. There were two offi-cers—both of them all puffed up like pigeons—and I told them I could see they were men of great authority and there was no good in arguing with them." His eyes twinkled over to Thomas. "At once I gave up two bags of . . . well, two bags."

"I'm sorry, Francis," Mama said sadly.

"Don't be, Mistress Virginia," Francis said with an impish grin. "They were both filled with rags and cinnamon!"

Papa shook his head as he put on his greatcoat. "I hope I can think of as easy a solution to what I have ahead, Francis," he said. "I'm off to the courthouse. That is where the militia headquarters is. I must take steps to free Nicholas."

As he was pulling on his gloves, there was a knock at the back door. Esther bustled to answer it and soon came back with a pale-faced young man on her heels.

Thomas's heart lurched. It was one of the Hutchinsons' servants—from the plantation. He looked disheveled and half-frozen, as if he had just ridden from Yorktown without stopping to take a breath. He wouldn't have done that unless something were very wrong at the homestead.

Everyone else was silent as the servant murmured in John Hutchinson's ear. Papa straightened up and looked around apologetically.

"Benedict Arnold has indeed paid our neighbors' plantation a visit," he said, "and burned down one of their barns. They took as much grain as they could load onto their small craft and sailed up the river with it."

To Thomas, Papa looked as if he were being torn in half.

"I have to go and see that our homestead is secured," Papa continued. "I will help Dr. Quincy after that."

So Malcolm went out to the stable to get Judge ready, and Thomas helped Francis put dovedung plasters on Papa's swollen arms and legs and rub tansy seed mixed with oil on his aching muscles.

"Who needs that useless hospital they've made out of the Palace?" Francis grumbled. "We've our own right here in this room!"

Papa chuckled even as he made his way to the front door.

"Oh, John," Mama said, clutching at him. "You must be careful. There has been so much trouble already!"

"I'll ride the back roads," Papa said. "The British know nothing of those."

And he slipped away into the darkness.

But the British, it seemed, had completed their work and were going to finish off their stay in Williamsburg with a round of raucous parties. The Hutchinsons, huddled around a sleeping Clayton in the parlor, could hear the shouting and drunken singing exploding from Wetherburn's, Chowning's, and the Raleigh.

"I hope they don't break any of Henry Wetherburn's Chinese porcelain," Clayton mumbled sleepily.

There was a tap at the front door, and everyone froze. Thomas could read the terror, even in Otis's eyes. It was the old man who, silent as always, went to peer out, and came back with Lydia Clark and Patsy in tow. Malcolm leaped to his sister and picked her up. She clung to his neck like a frightened squirrel.

"Lydia, my dear!" Mama said. "You look dreadful. What's happened?"

Mousy Lydia Clark indeed looked to Thomas as if she'd been chased there by a pack of wolves. Her hair stood out in wisps from her hooded cape, and her hazel eyes bulged from her small face like a possum's.

"Please forgive the intrusion."

"Don't be silly. What's happened?"

"I couldn't stay there. They threw a rock through our window!"

"Who?" Malcolm demanded. When it came to his little sister, his place as a servant was tossed aside.

"Those soldiers in their red coats!" Lydia cried. "You should see them. They're all out there reeling in the streets, drinking rum right out of the bottle and spilling it on themselves."

"Madmen," Francis muttered.

"Are you hurt, either of you?" Mama asked.

Malcolm had already done a thorough examination of Patsy.

Lydia shook her head. "Just frightened," she said. "I didn't know where else to go, and Patsy said we should come here. We'll sleep in the servants' quarters if you like."

"Don't be absurd!" Mama cried. "We've plenty of room right here in the house." She smiled a little, perhaps for the first time all day, Thomas thought. "You'd be hard put to get any of us to leave this parlor tonight, so there are plenty of bedrooms available upstairs."

But Lydia and Patsy stayed in the parlor, too. Patsy slept curled up on the hearth next to her brother, who never closed his eyes all night. Mama, Lydia, and Esther dozed in their chairs and woke now and then to reassure each other that all would be well. Otis stood guard by the door until he couldn't stand up any longer, and Esther clucked him to a stool. Francis and Thomas took turns giving Clayton his medicine until just before dawn when the oldest Hutchinson son fell into a deep, peaceful sleep.

"You go on and lie down now, Hutchinson," Francis whispered to Thomas. "It sounds like the British have all passed out, and Clayton is in the clear now. You get your rest."

Thomas crawled over to the hearth and stretched out on the rug. Murmuring softly in her sleep, Patsy stretched, and her hand landed on his cheek. He felt cozy and safe there, with two of his best friends so close by. But there was an empty place inside him, too, where Caroline should have been.

She would have had us all singing or playing games here tonight, Thomas thought. *But she can't. She's the enemy for sure now.*

Just before he drifted off, a tear rolled down from the corner of his eye.

The British rode out of Williamsburg the next day. Thomas watched from the back gate and smiled to himself. He wondered how long it would be before they discovered they had ridden off with bags of cinnamon and rags.

He spotted Malcolm striding toward him across the Palace Green, and Thomas could tell by the proud way he held his shoulders that he had news.

"I heard the men talking outside the courthouse when I was coming back from escorting Patsy and Lydia home," he said breathlessly. "Thomas Nelson and the militia are mad as wet roosters now. The British raided the magazine and took all the ammunition they weren't able to hide in time."

"Serves them right," Thomas said sourly. "They're keeping Nicholas in jail."

"But we still have a cause to fight for, lad."

Thomas turned his face and pouted. Malcolm crossed his arms over his chest and put his hands in his armpits to warm them. "War isn't fair to everyone," he said. "If we're going to win, we do need every able-bodied man to serve— especially doctors."

Thomas gnawed on the inside of his mouth.

"It makes enemies out of friends, too," he went on. "Robert Taylor had to turn on Francis Pickering. And Caroline . . . you have to know, lad, it will never be the same with her—"

"Shut it, Malcolm!" Thomas exploded. "You don't know everything!"

Malcolm shrugged and let his arms fall to his sides. "All right, then," he said. "I suppose you'll have to find it out for yourself."

In the next few days, everything changed again in Williamsburg. The streets grew deserted as every able-bodied man between 16 and 60 joined Thomas Nelson and his officers on the Palace and Courthouse Greens. From before dawn until long after sunset, the town was filled with the smell of wood smoke from the soldiers' fires. Roll call and inspection happened even before Thomas went to school, and all day the enlisted men in their fringed hunting shirts drilled under the direction of the blue-uniformed militia officers.

They were not nearly so grand as the British with all their shining brass, but Thomas noticed that there was something different about the militia now. Sam had always called them a motley crew of schoolboys being trained by the town bullies, but by the end of the first week of serious drilling, Thomas saw the same look in their eyes and the same straightness in their shoulders that the British had.

"Don't they look proud now?" Malcolm commented one evening as they watched the company of 400 men march up the Palace Green.

"I guess they do," Thomas said.

"It must be because they know what they're going to do."

"What *are* they going to do?"

"I heard this last market day when I passed some soldiers talking," Malcolm said. He leaned in and beckoned Thomas closer. "They're going to try to head off the British at Burwell's Ferry. We're going to have a battle very close by, lad."

Malcolm's black eyes shot sparks as if he could hardly stand the excitement. But Thomas felt a pang of fear go through him. He knew now that the very presence of the British could change things—important things.

The worst change, he decided later that night as he lay under his feather comforter trying to get warm enough to sleep, was that he hadn't seen Caroline since the afternoon she had come to warn them about Francis. He prayed about it every night, but so far God hadn't heard.

Please, God, he thought once again, *please don't let her be the enemy. I miss her.*

The one thing that didn't change after the British had come to Williamsburg was school. Every day Master Wrigley droned on and gave long, tedious assignments and watched for excuses to bring out the one-legged stool and the dunce cap. But everyone was being careful, and the next recitation day hadn't come yet.

But every day, the Terrible Trio filed into the classroom and shot warning looks at Thomas that clearly said, "Don't forget, if you ever show us up again, we'll get you."

Thomas wanted to fire looks back that said, "I'll get you first." But he didn't—because he wasn't sure he could. Caroline's idea of being the best scholar in the class hadn't worked. That was obvious. And there were three of them and only one of him. And Malcolm was too wrapped up in the war to even think about helping him anymore.

In fact, everyone was drifting away. There really wasn't a Fearsome Foursome any longer. So Thomas spent his days in smothering boredom, doing lessons he'd already learned with Alexander, and finding himself looking out the window at the naked trees, daydreaming about the days when he had studied with his beloved teacher and played behind the Governor's Palace with Caroline and worked for Francis and Nicholas.

He was doing that one afternoon—wishing he'd been the one instead of Malcolm to smuggle some of Francis's medicines back to him from the stable after the British left

—when he was aware that every eye in the room was on him.

He looked up to see Master Wrigley waving his riding crop in his direction. "You there!" he said. "Stand up and recite. Or are you not prepared?"

"No, sir, uh, yes, sir!" Thomas stammered as he got to his feet. *What was the question?* he thought in a panic. *Please give me the question again.*

"Well?" Master Wrigley said, impatiently tapping the pointy toe of his shoe.

"Sir?"

"You don't know, do you?"

"I don't know, sir. What was the—?"

But the sentence was never finished. With a triumphant flourish, Master Wrigley had the stool out from behind his desk, and Thomas was on it immediately. Thomas struggled to keep his balance.

"Now then!" the schoolteacher squeezed out through his nostrils. "You—come and recite!"

Zachary Digges made his way to the front of the room, and Thomas expected him to give him a smirk or a shove as he passed by. But Zachary stood before Master Wrigley and said, "I am not prepared either, sir. I beg your pardon."

Thomas thought Master Wrigley's wig was going to burst from his head. He bore down on the other two boys.

"Do you know the answer?" he shouted at Yancy.

Yancy shook his wide head without blinking an eye.

"And you?" he said to Kent Fitzhugh.

The handsome boy said, "No, sir."

Master Wrigley raised the crop high and cracked it down on the edge of his desk so hard that Thomas lost his balance and fell off the stool. But no one laughed. The only sound was Master Wrigley's screeching.

"You are a useless lot, and I have had all I can take of you! You are idiots, do you hear? Idiots!"

The "idiots" were all sent to their seats and given 100 Latin vocabulary words to learn and 20 ciphering problems to complete before five o'clock.

"There will be a written exam in two days!" Master Wrigley shouted over their heads. "So your fathers can see the ignorance they have bred!" And then he skulked back to his desk.

Thomas had never taken a written examination, and he wondered as he worked whether it was as shaming as reciting. Just in case it was, he wanted to be prepared. He was trying to figure out if 10 angels, blowing on 10 golden trumpets, are needed for each of the five continents to wake the dead on Judgment Day, how many angels the Lord must dispatch, when he heard a hissing sound from across the aisle.

He glanced up. Zachary Digges was mouthing something to him. Thomas looked warily at the front desk, but Master Wrigley sat with his arms folded and his eyes closed. His even, sleeping breathing set his shirt ruffle waving up and down. Thomas looked back at Zachary.

"How many angels?" Zachary whispered.

Thomas looked at him blankly. Before he knew quite what he was doing, he whispered back, "Fifty. Why?"

Zachary just smiled a straight-lipped smile and turned back to his copybook. The others nodded their heads at each other and scribbled down the answer.

It wasn't until after school when the three boys popped out from behind the hedge again that Thomas understood what was happening.

"You're smarter than I thought, Hutchinson!" Zachary said.

Kent nodded at his side, and Yancy snorted.

Thomas frowned and stomped his feet on the sidewalk to keep them from going numb. "What are you talking about?" he said.

"You took our warning seriously. You didn't show us up today. Good work."

"And you gave us the right answer to the ciphering problem," Kent put in, with the inevitable nod.

"How many angels on Judgment Day!" Yancy said. His ears seemed to flap as he shook his head. "What a stupid problem!"

Thomas stared from one of them to the other, and the light slowly began to dawn on him.

"You keep it up, Hutchinson, and you won't have to worry about anything from us," Zachary said. His lip curled as if he were enjoying the odor of day-old fish. "We can count on you, of course, to 'help' us on the written exam old Wiggly Wrigley announced today."

"'Help' you," Thomas said in a voice that came out flat. "You mean cheat."

"Call it what you will," Zachary said. He patted Thomas's

shoulder as if he were a five-year-old. "We know you'll cooperate. You've proven yourself."

Thomas jerked his shoulder away, and Zachary laughed harshly. Kent and Yancy chimed in as they followed their leader off down the sidewalk.

Thomas was left alone on the corner, shivering with anger.

✝ ✝ ✝

Thomas was still seething when he slammed the front door of his house behind him. A head with a big, curled wig on it stuck out the parlor door and its owner, Mistress Wetherburn, gave him a disapproving "Shhh!"

The head disappeared inside the parlor again, and as the door closed, Thomas got a glimpse of a circle of ladies in billowing skirts sitting with their heads bowed and their hands folded in their laps. He could hear Mama's sweet voice murmuring softly.

Thomas wandered to the back of the house, where Otis was emerging from Papa's library with an empty tea tray.

"What is happening in the parlor?" Thomas said to him.

"They're a-prayin'," Otis grunted, and went out the back door.

Thomas's anger had been replaced by curiosity and, overcome with it, he went to the library and looked in. Clayton had not powdered his hair that morning, and his tawny head was glowing in the light of his candle as he bent over a piece of paper and a quill pen at Papa's desk.

He certainly looks different from Papa sitting there, Thomas thought. *He's so small and frail and gray-eyed.*

Clayton looked up absently. "Oh," he said. "Good day, Thomas. Come in. Have some tea?"

Thomas looked back to be sure it was really him Clayton was talking to. He didn't like bee balm tea, but he went in anyway and sat on the edge of the chair facing the desk.

"Why are all those women praying in the parlor?" he asked.

Clayton stopped writing to dip his pen in the inkpot. "Mama gathered them together. She said she could feel the power of people praying together that night Papa came home from Richmond. She wants to do something, and she says it can't hurt to have the ladies on God's side."

"Oh," Thomas said. "She said she was tired of being helpless."

"You're never helpless when you go to God for guidance," Clayton said, as if he'd pulled a handle for the right answer. He began writing again.

Thomas squirmed in the chair. The pen scratched across the paper.

"What are you doing?" he said finally.

"I'm writing some letters to try to help Nicholas Quincy," Clayton said. "I can't let them force him to go to war when God has clearly told him not to."

"Who are you writing to?" Thomas said.

"Governor Jefferson in Charlottesville. John Adams, Benjamin Franklin, some of the others."

"Oh!" Thomas said. Those were names his father had been speaking of in reverent tones ever since the struggle for independence had started. And Clayton—weak, sickly, grouchy Clayton—was writing to them. Nicholas was never going to get out of jail.

Thomas felt a wave of restlessness and left the library. Clayton grunted softly and kept writing.

He wandered out to the kitchen building, where Esther was packing a basket with two jars of chicken soup and several loaves of bread. Although Thomas didn't give it a second glance, she stopped to shake a finger at him.

"Don't you be a-thinkin' any of this is for you, Thomas Hutchinson," she said. "You would eat this very tabletop if it weren't nailed down."

"I'm not hungry," Thomas said.

Malcolm looked up from the harness he was repairing by the fire and studied Thomas's face. "Are you sick, then, lad?"

Thomas scowled at him and sat down on the hearth. "No," he said. "Just bored."

Esther tucked a cloth over the contents of the basket and wiped her hands on her apron. "All you ever have to do is ask me," she said. "I can always find something for you to do!"

Malcolm caught Thomas's eye and smiled a half-grin. Thomas rolled his eyes.

"Right now you can deliver this basket for me," she clucked on. "They don't feed them well in the jail, and some of the other servants in town and I have decided if we want the good doctor alive when Clayton gets him set free, we'd best be feedin' him ourselves."

"Nicholas?" Thomas said, scrambling up from the hearth. "You're taking that to Nicholas Quincy?"

"No," she said, holding out the basket. "You are."

"I'd like to go with him, Esther, if I may," Malcolm said. "I've finished my work here."

"Go," Esther said, dismissing them both with the flapping of her apron. "You can make sure Thomas doesn't sample any of this on his way there. I want Dr. Quincy to have every dumplin' in that soup, mind you."

She was still talking when the two boys left the kitchen.

As they made their way down Nicholson Street toward the jail, Thomas tried not to look up at the Taylors' house. Malcolm, however, couldn't ignore it.

"I heard Robert Taylor had British officers stayin' right in his spare bedroom," Malcolm said.

"That's rot!" Thomas said. "Where did you hear that?"

"From Patsy," Malcolm said.

"Oh."

"They still go about together, she and Caroline."

Thomas impatiently shifted the basket to his other hand. "Why would Caroline still be friends with Patsy and not me?"

Malcolm gave a grunt. "Patsy doesn't act as if she suspects Caroline were guilty of some horrible crime every time she sees her."

"I don't do that!"

"It's certain you do, lad. That day she came to tell us that the British were after Francis Pickering's medicine, you acted like she might have the plague!"

Thomas slowed down to answer, but Malcolm suddenly doubled his speed.

"What are you doing?" Thomas said.

"Don't turn around, lad," Malcolm said out of the side of his square mouth. "I think we're being followed."

"What?" Thomas said. "By who?" He started to glance over his shoulder, but Malcolm poked him in the side.

"Don't look!"

"Who is it?" Thomas hissed.

"I don't know. But I've been hearing twigs snap at every corner, like someone is trailin' us in the woods there."

"How can you—?"

"You forget my father was a thief," Malcolm said. "He taught me how to tell if the town officials were on to us."

Thomas was dying to turn around and look. As if he knew it, Malcolm put a firm hand on his elbow.

"Who would be following us?" Thomas whispered.

Malcolm got the know-it-all look in his eye. "Could be anyone, lad. Those three ruffians in your class at school, perhaps."

Thomas did look around then, and Malcolm grabbed his arm and yanked him into the carpenter's yard.

"What are we doing here?" Thomas said.

"Gettin' you out of sight before they see that we know they're there!" Malcolm said. He brought up one corner of his mouth. "I can see I have a lot to teach you about avoidin' capture."

Thomas hitched his arm away and scowled. "Capture? Who would care to capture me?"

"Your school bullies—"

"Pooh!"

"Or Xavier Wormeley, if he finds out you helped Francis hide the medicine from his soldiers."

Thomas's eyes met Malcolm's sharp black ones.

"Oh," he said.

"Or a British soldier they left behind to spy. We did say we were goin' to join the British army, you remember."

Thomas felt a chill go up his spine, and he shivered. Malcolm patted him on the shoulder.

"But you don't have to get caught, lad," he said. "Not if you learn from me."

Thomas nodded solemnly.

Malcolm peered out onto the street and then said, "I think it's safe now. Let's go."

Thomas's heart hammered painfully in his throat all the way to the jail, and he kept his neck stiff so he wouldn't look behind him.

But once Peter Pelham, the jailer, let them into Nicholas's cell, all fears of his own disappeared into the darkness of the damp, smelly hole.

Thomas had actually spent the night in a cell before, but it had been warm then and empty except for himself and Papa. Now the jail was crammed with men, and it smelled as if most of them had been in there for a long time.

"Who are all these people?" Thomas whispered to Malcolm.

"Deserters, some of them," Malcolm whispered back. "Spies, maybe."

Thomas thought of Alexander and shuddered.

They found Nicholas against the wall under the window with a thin, filthy prisoner who blended in so well with the dreariness of the cell that all Thomas could really see were his glazed eyes. But Nicholas's pale-blue eyes danced to life when he saw them, and he stood up to pull them both into a hug. Thomas felt himself clinging to him.

"Come, sit down," Nicholas said. His voice sounded as calm and shy as ever. He kicked some straw into a pile for a seat. "I'm sorry I have nothing to offer you."

"It's us who have something for you," Malcolm said. "Though I'm not sure you'll thank us. Esther made it."

Nicholas chuckled softly as he took the basket from Thomas. Its cover was wrinkled from Peter Pelham's search, but Nicholas lifted it as if it were the finest linen.

"It has to be better than anything they serve here," the doctor said. "Starvation would be healthier."

Thomas and Malcolm huddled next to him on the floor. Thomas noticed that in the frightening darkness of the cell, the know-it-all look had disappeared from Malcolm's face. It looked as pinched and white as Thomas's felt.

"Have they beaten the bottoms of your feet with a birch cane?" Thomas asked.

Malcolm gave him a hard nudge.

"No," Nicholas said, "but they've threatened me with branding or cutting off one of my feet if I don't agree to serve."

"They're all talk!" Malcolm cried. "They'll never do that!"

There was a miserable silence, until the glassy-eyed man coughed. "This is Mr. Phelps," Nicholas said, nodding to him. "I've just been having a look at his throat." Nicholas shook his head. "Sickness runs rampant here. I can't do much for them, though, without any medicines or supplies."

"You're doctoring—in here?" Malcolm asked.

"Doctoring is my gift from God," Nicholas said. "He's directed me to use it wherever I am."

"Maybe we could bring you your bag next time we come," Thomas said. "What medicines do you need?"

Nicholas's pale eyes widened. "Are there any left? The talk I've overheard here is that the British made off with it all."

Malcolm snickered. "They made off with two bags of nothing, thanks to Thomas!" He told Nicholas the story of Francis and Thomas's trick on the British.

Nicholas smiled at Thomas proudly. "You're a smart one, young Hutchinson."

"Dr. Quincy?" said a quavery voice.

They all looked up at a trembling figure standing over them with a rag tied around his arm.

"Yes, Mr. Franks?"

"This wound is painin' me considerable, sir. Is there anything you can do?"

Nicholas guided the shaking man to the floor and unwrapped the rag from his arm. Thomas realized it was part of his shirtsleeve that he'd torn off. Nicholas unwrapped it, and Thomas gagged. Malcolm pulled his jacket up over his nose. The wound stank as if it had been packed with pork nine days old.

"It needs washing again," Nicholas said. "I have a little water left." He reached into his jacket and pulled out a flask, which he held over the wound until a few drops of water trickled out. He then took off his jacket and put it around Mr. Franks's shoulders. The man stopped shivering as Nicholas ripped off the bottom of his own sleeve and rewrapped the ugly wound.

"Now, then," he said, smiling his faint smile. "I think I have something that will make you forget your sickness for a while—you, too, Mr. Phelps." He pulled a jar of soup out of the basket. "Nourishment can go a long way toward healing."

Thomas and Malcolm watched helplessly as Nicholas poured chicken and dumpling soup into the tankard Esther had tucked in and handed it to Mr. Phelps. He took a grateful swallow and handed it to Mr. Franks.

"There's bread here for the rest of you!" Nicholas said to the cell. "Some decent food might keep you from becoming my patients, too, eh?"

They were suddenly surrounded by smelly, whiskered men whose gaunt faces broke into smiles as they took hunks of bread from Nicholas and stuffed them into their mouths. Thomas thought he could hear their dry lips cracking as they chewed.

Without his jacket, Nicholas shuddered in the dreary cell. Thomas edged closer to him. He wanted to put his arm around the doctor's shoulders, but he couldn't get it to move.

"Why don't you just do what Xavier Wormeley wants so you don't have to stay here?" he whispered instead.

Nicholas cocked his head at him, the way he'd done a hundred times when they'd talked. "What are you saying, Thomas?"

"You could say you'd serve with the militia, and then you could just . . . run away!"

Nicholas looked at him closely. "Lie?"

"Malcolm and I had to lie to keep those soldiers from stealing Burgess or finding out that the family was in the house! Malcolm told you Francis and I fooled the British, and you thought that was all right."

Nicholas rubbed his forehead. "Running away is something entirely different," he said finally. "I cannot run away from my own conscience, and it is a person's conscience that tells him what God wants. The only freedom is in doing what God tells me is right."

"But haven't you prayed, Nicholas?" Thomas said. "Haven't you told Him what you want?"

"I seldom tell God what I want, Thomas," he said. "I wait for Him to tell me what He wants."

"What is He telling you now?" Malcolm asked.

Thomas had almost forgotten Malcolm was there. But he was very much there, leaning forward, his black eyes alive.

"That my place right now is here, with Mr. Phelps and Mr. Franks. There are others—men like your father, Thomas—whose place it is to soften the hearts of Xavier Wormeley and the militia."

Thomas swallowed hard. "Papa had to go to our plantation . . ." His voice trailed off. He didn't say that Clayton was writing letters. Without Papa, surely there was no chance.

"I'm not worried," Nicholas said. "God always provides."

"I hope He provides before the militia leaves for Burwell's Ferry," Malcolm said fiercely. "Or they'll be draggin' you with them!"

Nicholas sighed. "Then it seems I must pray and find out what the Lord would have me do, eh?"

Peter Pelham's keys jangled outside the door, and Malcolm pulled on Thomas's arm and stood up. "Come on, Thomas," he said. "We have to go."

Thomas got up slowly. He wanted to get out of this rank and dismal place. But he didn't want to leave Nicholas. Even here, there was always peace around him—as if he always knew what to do.

Outside, in a gray light that seemed bright compared to the mournful blackness of the cell, Malcolm took hold of Thomas's arm.

"I made a decision in there, lad," Malcolm said. "When the militia goes to Burwell's Ferry, I'm going to go and watch."

"Why?" Thomas said.

"I don't rightly know yet," he said. He looked at Thomas with fire in his eyes. "But I think it's my conscience telling me to."

✢ ✢ ✢

Chapter Fourteen

Thomas listlessly turned the pages of his copybook in the parlor that night, but his mind was far from the next day's written examination. There had been a time, he thought, when the fear of his father seeing the ignorance he had bred would have been the heaviest trouble on his shoulders.

It would have been right up there on the list with what was going to happen to him if he didn't help Zachary, Yancy, and Kent with the answers. And what would happen to him if Master Wiggly Wrigley caught him if he did.

But now the fears that flickered in his head like flames made those seem childish and lame.

Everyone he knew was in trouble.

Sam was out there running from Cornwallis.

Alexander was risking his life spying—for someone. And

because of it—because of the whole war—Caroline was now the enemy.

Francis had to get his medicines and herbs from the Hutchinsons' stable as he needed them, so Xavier Wormeley wouldn't find out they hadn't all gone to the British. Papa was at the plantation dodging the British, and Nicholas sat in that horrible jail, where he gave away everything he had to men who were even worse off than he was.

And what can any of us do about any of it? Thomas thought. He looked around the parlor at the heads bent over their evening business. Ever since the British had been there, they'd all huddled together after Evening Prayer, even the servants. They were all that was left behind to handle everything . . . sickly Clayton, who only had enough strength to sit in the library and write letters . . . and Mama, who sat in the parlor every afternoon and prayed with a bunch of ladies . . . and Esther, who fussed over her longer than Thomas could listen to her . . . and old Otis, who never said anything at all. The only one strong and smart enough to really do anything to help was Malcolm, and he was wasting his time dreaming about following the Williamsburg militia to Burwell's Ferry.

I've prayed and prayed, Thomas thought. *But it doesn't seem like God is listening. Things are only getting worse.*

That thought rubbed against him like a scratchy homespun shirt. Something about it wasn't right . . . but what? Was it something Nicholas had said?

"That must be a hateful lesson you're studying, Thomas. You're frowning like a judge."

Thomas looked up at Clayton, who was watching him curiously from the desk in the corner where he was ensconced with his letter writing.

"No," Thomas mumbled. "It's only Latin vocabulary."

"Oh," Mama said. She laughed a little bell-laugh. "It sounds hateful to me!"

"May I see?" Clayton asked.

Thomas held out the copybook to him. Clayton's gray eyes passed over it.

"That's what Master Wiggly—I mean *Wrigley*—is examining us on tomorrow," Thomas said.

"You're having an examination, then," Clayton said. "Shall we see how ready you are?"

Thomas shrugged.

Clayton looked at the copybook. "*Vita,*" he said.

"Life," Thomas answered.

"*Vis.*"

"Strength."

Clayton looked over the top of the book into Thomas's eyes. "*Honos.*"

"Honor," Thomas said.

His brother sat gazing at him for so long that Thomas began to squirm.

"That was right, wasn't it?" Thomas said finally.

"Yes, very right," Clayton said. "You've studied hard this evening."

"No," Thomas said. "I learned those last summer with Alexander."

Clayton's mouth came open slightly, and he handed the

copybook back to him. "You should do well on your examination, Thomas. Father will be proud."

"We're all proud, Thomas!" Mama said. "It is so fine to have something good to think about for a change!" She set down her sewing as if she'd just made a decision. "We must celebrate!" she said. "All the ladies brought treats to our prayer meeting today, and there is so much left over. Esther, we must have a party!"

No one protested, and within minutes Otis had moved the drop-leaf table to the middle of the parlor, Malcolm had stoked the fire to a cheery blaze, and Esther had produced a tall pile of desserts, a tray of scalloped oysters, and six steaming cups of chocolate.

Thomas had just popped two brown sugar cakes with pecans into his mouth when Mama said, "Let us drink to our brilliant scholar, shall we?"

Everyone held their cups high—even Clayton—and cried, "Here, here!"

Cheeks bulging, Thomas couldn't help but smile . . . and maybe even believe them a little.

But that was hard to remember the next day as he sat in his hard seat in the chilly schoolroom while Master Wrigley made a production of placing the examinations facedown on the desktops.

"You will be lucky to pass this test, considering your work thus far," the schoolmaster said. "Do not even consider cheating, because I will be watching you all like a hawk."

Thomas didn't look at Zachary, but he knew he was looking at him, probably with his upper lip curled to his forehead.

Master Wiggly isn't as clueless as we thought, Thomas said to himself. *I'm going to have to be careful not to even look their way.*

"You may begin," the teacher said. "And remember, I will be watching."

He did one of his military turns and marched to his desk. Thomas turned his paper over and read the first question. Easy. And the second one, too. His eyes ran down the page, and he stifled a smile. There was nothing on it that Alexander hadn't taught him months ago. He dipped his pen in his inkwell.

"Psst!" came a sound from the next row.

Thomas just kept writing.

"Wiggly is sleeping!" the voice hissed.

Thomas let his eyes dart to the front of the room. Sure enough, the teacher sat with his ridiculous wig bobbing over an open book. A trail of drool slid from the corner of his mouth.

"Number one," Zachary whispered. "What is the answer?"

But Thomas kept his eyes and his pen firmly on his test paper and wrote the answer to number 10.

Zachary cleared his throat impatiently. Thomas answered 11, 12, 13, 14.

Zachary coughed again and then dropped his quill pen to the floor and leaned out to pick it up. His face even with Thomas's knee, he hissed, "Answer me, Hutchinson!"

Thomas's heart was drumming furiously, but he dug his

eyes into his paper and answered 15, 16, and 17. Three more Latin nouns to go, and then five ciphering problems. His pen flew across the page.

Zachary retrieved his from the floor with a savage grab and sat back up in his seat. He gave one last long cough. Thomas could feel Kent and Yancy squirming anxiously, and out of the corner of his eye, he saw them giving quick little glances over their shoulders. He finished the nouns and started the arithmetic.

Zachary drew in enough breath to suffocate the room and whispered hoarsely, "Give—me—the—answer—or —you'll—be—sorry!"

Master Wrigley startled awake and looked around the room with confused eyes. Thomas went back to his paper and wrote the answer to how many pokeberries the farmer's wife had to gather to dye 100 yards of thread if it took one quart of pokeberries for every 20 yards of thread. He could hear the schoolteacher coming down the aisle, tapping his riding crop against his breeches. He seemed to stop at every desk, where he sniggered with satisfaction. Thomas completed the second ciphering problem.

When he saw Master Wrigley's shadow fall across his desk, he clutched his pen tightly and kept writing. If John the Baptist was beheaded in 32 A.D. and the book of Revelation was written in 87 A.D., John the Baptist was beheaded 55 years before the book—

He heard Master Wrigley gasp, and he looked up. The teacher was gazing down at his paper as if it were a rattle-snake coiled to strike. Thomas searched his paper to see if he'd smeared his ink or made his capital J wrong. When he looked up again, the teacher had turned on his heel and stalked back to his desk. His wig went crooked, and he reached up and snatched it back into place and sat down. He stared at Thomas and vibrated the riding crop on his desktop.

He wants to hit me with that, Thomas thought, his heart vibrating just as fast. *What did I do wrong?*

He gulped and went back to his test paper. Whatever it was, it was too late now. There was nothing to do but finish the test. He read the next problem and his heart sank. "The schoolmaster punished John for soiling his book. He gave him 3 blows on one ear and 3 blows on the other ear. How many blows did John receive?"

"John received 6 blows," Thomas wrote—and hoped he would receive only that many.

But when their time was up, Master Wrigley collected the papers without a word and dismissed them all early for dinner. Thomas hurried to get out of the room before the teacher could call him back, and he was almost to the corner of the college yard when he heard the sound of thundering feet approaching from behind.

He didn't have to look back to know who it was. He broke into a run—and was knocked down within two steps.

Yancy Byrd was suddenly in front of him, pinning his arms, and he could feel Kent's grasp on his ankles. He groaned as Zachary sat astride his back and yanked back his head by his hair.

"Let go of me!" Thomas cried. "Get off!"

He managed to rip his arms away from Yancy's pudgy fingers, but Zachary shoved his face into the half-frozen slush on the ground, and Yancy was able to grab hold again. It was obvious he couldn't get away from all three of them, and the thought burned up his backbone like a wildfire. He kicked his foot hard and felt it connect with something.

"Ow!" Kent screamed. "He got me in the chin!"

"Smack him, then!" Zachary cried.

Kent did, across Thomas's calf. Thomas lay still and boiled.

"I thought you knew what to do, Hutchinson!" Zachary said. "Didn't you study for us? Didn't you know the answers?"

"I knew every answer on the test—idiot!" Thomas shouted.

"Then why didn't you give them to me? Wiggly was asleep the entire time. You could have given us every one!"

"I'm not a filthy cheater like you are!"

He felt Zachary's weight come off his back, but before he could move, it came down on him again with a bone-breaking bounce. It knocked the air out of Thomas, and he had to gasp for it. When he did, a pain tore through his left side. For the first time since they'd dumped him on the ground, he was afraid.

"*What* am I?" Zachary yelled close to his ear. "*What* did you say I am?"

Please, God, Thomas started to pray. But he didn't know what to say next. He couldn't think what God could possibly do except strike all three of them dead right there.

What should I do, God? he prayed desperately. *What can I do?*

"You wouldn't answer me in class because you're *afraid* of Master Wiggly!" Zachary cried. "But you're going to answer me now, if I have to beat it out of you!"

Something hard—like a fist—came down on Thomas's left shoulder, and he choked back a scream.

"Don't just sit there, ninnies!" Zachary growled. "Get him! Get him good!"

Thomas felt his foot being grabbed and his leg being twisted until it felt as if his knee would burst. In front of him, Yancy took a bite out of his forearm.

Thomas wrenched his arm away and doubled his fist, but Zachary grabbed it and pulled it behind him . . . and kept pulling.

"Stop!" was all Thomas could cry. "Stop it, please!"

And then it was as if his voice were two—and one of them was saying, "Stop it! Get off him at once before I flatten your bloody heads!"

Yancy was the first to let go, and then Kent. Zachary had to be pried off him, and Thomas heard his skinny body hit the ground before he yelped. Three sets of running footsteps disappeared across the yard.

"Thomas, are you all right, lad?" he heard someone say.

When his body was turned over, he looked up into the sharp black eyes of Malcolm Donaldson.

✜ ⬥ ✜

Chapter Fifteen

ll Thomas could do was groan.

"What are you saying?" Malcolm asked.

"Thank you, God," Thomas said. And then every-thing went black.

The next thing he remembered was Francis Pickering's wheezing voice somewhere above him.

"How did you ever carry him here?" he was saying. "He's half again your weight."

"They say fear does that for you, sir," Malcolm said. "I once saw a Scotsman lift an entire horse that had fallen on his son."

Thomas's eyes fluttered open, and he looked at Malcolm. "You're making that up, Malcolm," he said. "You never saw any such thing."

Malcolm's face broke into a square smile, and he grabbed

Thomas's hand. Thomas moaned.

"That hurts, too, eh, boy?" Francis said.

"Everything hurts," Thomas said.

Francis clicked his tongue sympathetically. "Don't you worry. We'll get you patched up. I'll need some things, though." He looked across the examining-room table at Malcolm. "You stay here with him and keep these warm towels on him. I'll take the wagon and fetch what I need from your stable." He scowled over his spectacles. "That woman of yours won't come after me, will she?"

Malcolm chuckled. "I think Esther will leave you alone, sir."

Francis nodded and started to skitter out.

"No big plasters and such, sir," Thomas said. "Papa can't know I've been fighting, and neither can Clayton. He's sure to tell Papa."

"I don't think you have much choice, Hutchinson," Francis wheezed. "It will take a miracle to patch you up without plasters and slings and everything else I have." He moved toward the door. "Young ruffians do more damage than the militia. They have their own war going."

He shut the door behind him, and Thomas moaned loudly. "Papa is going to be so angry with me. He has forbidden me to fight."

"Don't be an idiot, lad!" Malcolm said. "You weren't fightin'! There were three of them, and they had you flat on the ground. You couldn't have fought if you wanted to!"

"I am an idiot. I should have just cheated like they told me to."

"But it was God told you not to, I'll be bound. What did Dr. Quincy call that?"

"Conscience," Thomas said.

"What he said the other day in the jail, that made more sense to me than any sermon I ever heard in church. That's why I'm going to Burwell's Ferry. My conscience won't let me stay home."

Thomas tried to nod, but it hurt too much. He could feel one of his eyes swelling with every throb.

"You're going to have a shiner too big for any plaster to cover, I'll warrant you," Malcolm said, "and a knee the size of a spring ham." He ran a finger gently over Thomas's arm. "What happened here?"

"Yancy bit me," Thomas said.

"Animal," Malcolm said.

"It's a good thing you happened along. Do you think they'd have killed me?"

Malcolm looked a little puzzled. "I didn't actually 'happen along,' lad. Patsy came runnin' into the laundry where I was helpin' Esther wash the bed linens and told me I had to come because she'd seen three boys a-beatin' you to a bloody pulp in the school yard."

"What was she doing there?" Thomas said.

"I didn't stop to ask her. I knew if it was those same three who threw the rock at Caroline, I'd better be gettin' there fast. To them, this is not a game like we play."

Thomas let out a sigh and then gasped. The worst pain yet ripped through his left side. He remembered when that happened, when Zachary had jumped on him.

"What is it, lad?" Malcolm said. He stood up over the table, both arms held helplessly in midair. "What hurts? What would you have me do?"

"My side," Thomas said. "It feels like it's going to burst!"

"What do I do?"

The shop door jangled open, and Malcolm looked as if he'd cry with relief. "Mr. Pickering is back. He'll know what to do."

But it wasn't Francis who appeared in the doorway.

It was Nicholas.

"Dr. Quincy!" Malcolm said. "How did you—? Can you do somethin'—? Thomas, he's—"

Nicholas went straight to the table and put his gentle hands on Thomas's side. Thomas gasped, but he couldn't stop smiling.

"What are you *doing* here, sir? How did you get out?"

"I'm not sure of that myself," Nicholas said. He pressed lightly. "Does that hurt?"

"Yes!"

"All right, then. We'll push there no more, eh?" He looked around the room. "Has Francis any comfrey to make a poultice? I think we have a broken rib here, Thomas."

"He should be back with medicine directly," Malcolm said. "We're still hidin' it in the stable for fear of Xavier Wormeley."

Nicholas shook his head. "It's bad enough we've the British to trouble us. But now the men on our own side have become our enemies."

"Why did Xavier change his mind about you?" Malcolm

said as Nicholas ran his hands tenderly down Thomas's legs.

Thomas could feel the pain ebbing away at his very touch.

"He didn't," Nicholas said. "It was Peter Pelham who escorted me out of the jail cell and told me to stay out of sight until *Captain* Wormeley cooled down. Mr. Pelham just said the courthouse had sent word that I was to be released."

"And not a moment too soon! Nicholas!" Francis scurried from the door and clasped Nicholas's hands in his.

Their faces glowed, and Thomas thought, *I never knew they were such good friends.* He suddenly missed Caroline, and it hurt worse than any of his injuries.

But he bit back the tears and looked at the three of them, who were also his friends. Nicholas was there with them again and Malcolm had saved him from the Terrible Trio and Francis was already making plasters for him.

God must be listening at last, Thomas thought. *He must be answering my prayers like I asked Him to.*

Yet something about that still bothered him. Something about conscience.

But it disappeared as he felt himself growing sleepy. He let his eyes drift closed for just a second. The next thing he knew, he was opening them to the parlor and a cheerful fire in the fireplace and Mama's soothing voice close to his face.

"He's coming back to us from that good sleep," she said.

Thomas tried to smile at her, but his face was stiff.

"My baby boy, looking as if he'd been in a tavern brawl," she said.

He closed his eyes and heard Malcolm snicker.

I'll get him for that later, Thomas thought. *I'm too tired now.*

The next time he woke up, he smelled venison stew, and he lifted his head to sniff.

"You lie yourself right back down, boy," Esther said, giving his chest a gentle shove. But even she was smiling, her face a wreath of soft wrinkles and folds. "He's feelin' better. He's a-goin' after the food."

"Let him eat all he wants," Nicholas said. "It will be good for the healing."

"I'll get him a bowl," Malcolm said. "Lydia Clark sent it over, Thomas, to thank us for the night she and Patsy spent here." He leaned in close to Thomas's ear and added, "So it's safe to eat!"

While Malcolm ladled stew into a porringer for him, Thomas looked around the room. It was almost dark, and Otis was piling more wood into the fireplace, Esther was bustling about, and Nicholas was sitting between Mama and Clayton, selecting a piece of sponge cake from the tray Mama was tempting him with.

"We're having a party, Thomas," Mama said. "To celebrate Malcolm's saving you, and Dr. Quincy's release from jail!"

"I could celebrate with more joy," Nicholas said with his farm-boy shyness, "if I could thank the person who was responsible for my freedom."

"Why don't we go straight to the source and just thank God for the law?" Clayton said.

"What I would like to know," Esther said, "if you don't mind, sir—"

Clayton nodded to her.

"I would like to know what is to be done with those three hoodlums who did this to our Thomas."

"It's certain there should be a punishment," Clayton said.

"But I am sure John would like some say in this," Mama said nervously.

Everyone nodded in agreement, Thomas saw—except Malcolm. His face grew dark, and Thomas was sure he saw a plan brewing in his eyes.

The stew *was* delicious, but before long, Thomas's eyes grew heavy again.

"Don't you want to stay with us tonight, Nicholas?" he heard Clayton say as he drifted off. "I don't trust Xavier Wormeley for a minute."

"No," Dr. Quincy said. "Hiding is the same as running. I must have my freedom honestly."

"I admire your courage," Clayton said.

After that, Esther and Malcolm hauled Thomas off to bed, and that was where he stayed for the next five days. Nicholas came each morning to change the plasters and check his rib and tell him the latest stories about their Williamsburg patients.

"Mistress Wetherburn is convinced she caught some strange fever from the British when they were here," Nicholas told him, chuckling. "She says it has caused her face to puff up."

"Too many apple tarts is what has made her face puff up!" Thomas said.

Nicholas laughed until his pale-blue eyes shined. "I've

missed your company in my doctoring," he said.

Esther and Mama fussed over him frequently, but it was Clayton who surprised Thomas. He hobbled up the stairs several times a day to bring him books to read or warn him what to avoid on Esther's meal trays. Thomas waited for him to scold him for provoking the Terrible Trio into a fight, but he never did. He only asked one question.

"Why did those boys attack you, Thomas?" he said the second day.

Thomas looked uncomfortably at his quilt. *Should I tell him they wanted me to cheat? Or am I asking for more trouble if I do that? I do have to go back to school and face them someday.*

"They said I showed them up in the classroom," Thomas said slowly. "Because I knew the answer in recitation and they didn't."

"What is it they wanted you to do?"

"Refuse to give the right answers, like they did," Thomas said.

"I find that truly the most absurd thing I have ever heard of!" Clayton cried. His pale face was blotchy. "Who are the parents of such children?"

Thomas knew he was gaping at him, but he couldn't help himself.

"Those boys have obviously had no training," Clayton went on. "No proper upbringing. Not like you have."

In a daze, Thomas shook his head. He wasn't sure, but he thought Clayton was defending *him.*

Clayton shook his head and put his hand lightly on

Thomas's shoulder. "Papa will, of course, decide what's to be done when he returns, but in the meantime, I think we should pray for all of them, eh?"

Thomas nodded. "What do we ask for?"

"For God's guidance. He'll direct us in the right way."

When he left, Thomas lay thinking about that for a long time. No one else—well, at least not Clayton or Nicholas—seemed to pray the way he did. He was always asking for things that, frankly, God didn't come through with. But they talked about listening for God's direction and following God's guidance. That did seem different somehow.

On the sixth day of resting, Thomas grew so fidgety that he sneaked out of bed when he was supposed to be napping and went carefully to the window. It didn't hurt when he walked or when he breathed, and it felt better to be away from his featherbed and his quilt. He stretched cautiously and looked out the window.

The militia was drilling on the Palace Green. As he watched them march back and forth in their straight lines, something caught his eye, closer to his house.

It was Caroline's red capuchin.

She was standing beside their front gate, and she, too, seemed to be watching the soldiers prepare for battle.

He felt a pain that didn't come from any of his wounds or bruises. It throbbed in the middle of his chest. It was the longing to run downstairs and join her . . . to play guessing games with her about what the soldiers' names were and what kinds of adventures they'd had in getting their guns and horses to fight in the war . . . to have her call him "Tom" . . . to be her friend again.

The sob that came from his throat surprised even him.

As the soldiers made their turn at the end of the Green, Caroline turned, too, and looked up at Thomas's window. Her brown eyes—that seemed to fill up the top half of her face—grew even rounder when she saw him. But her slice-of-melon smile didn't appear. She looked as sad as he felt.

Thomas pulled away from the window and climbed back into bed.

He had a hard time falling asleep that night, even after Mama brought him a posset and Esther fluffed up his cushions and comforter. Every time he closed his eyes, he saw Caroline's sad eyes, and he hurt all over because he hadn't laughed with her in such a long time.

Dear God, he prayed, *why does she have to be the enemy?*

He wasn't sure he had been to sleep at all when suddenly there was someone standing next to his bed, gently shaking him.

"Thomas, lad," Malcolm whispered to him. "Wake up."

Thomas sat up and rubbed his eyes. "What is it? What's wrong?"

"The militia is gathered on the Green, ready to go."

"Go where?"

"To Burwell's Ferry. Tonight is the night!"

Thomas knew he was awake then. "Are you going with them?"

"Yes, I am. I thought someone should know where I'd gone, just in case—"

"In case what?"

"What do you think, lad? It's a battle."

He gave Thomas's shoulder a pat and turned to go.

But Thomas couldn't watch another of his friends go out the door. He scrambled from the bed with his heart nearly breaking.

"Malcolm!" he whispered.

"What is it, lad?"

"Don't go—please! You'll never come back!"

Malcolm scowled and stuck his face into Thomas's. "Don't be an idiot, lad!" he hissed. "Of course I'm coming back. Now get back in bed before we have Esther bustlin' through here."

"No!" Thomas whispered hoarsely. He swallowed—hard. "If you're going to go, then I'm coming with you. And you can't stop me!"

✢ ✢ ✢

Chapter Sixteen

Malcolm pulled his face back as if Thomas had just spit in it.

"What?"

"Everyone is gone!" Thomas whispered. "I can't be left behind anymore. I have to go with you!" He snatched up his warmest breeches, shirt, vest, and jacket from his cabinet and began to put them on.

Malcolm stood with his hands on his hips and his eyes blazing. "You're still too weak, lad—"

"I've been in bed for six days! How weak can I be? I tell you, I'm well!"

"You'll only slow me down."

"I will if I wake up Clayton and Otis and tell them you've gone!"

One of Malcolm's eyebrows went up. The rest of him

went still. "Are you threatening me, Thomas Hutchinson?"

Thomas looked up from the woolen stocking he was pulling on. "Yes," he said, "I am." He went for the door. "Are you ready then?"

Malcolm sighed and followed him down the back stairs.

"If anything happens to you, your papa will turn me out on the high road!" he hissed after him.

Thomas was ready for that one, too. His spirits were already beginning to lift. "You won't let anything happen to me. And if anything does, I'll tell Papa it wasn't your fault. I'm free to do what my conscience tells me is right, too, you know."

Malcolm couldn't answer. He sighed darkly and stomped toward the stable.

"Which horse are we taking?" Thomas whispered.

"Musket. I have no right to take your papa's—"

"I'm giving you permission to take Burgess. He's my horse, too. I'm a Hutchinson." Thomas could see the gleam in Malcolm's eye. "Now aren't you glad you're taking me?"

Malcolm grunted and tossed a blanket across Burgess's back.

In minutes, they had him saddled and were clomping quietly toward Burwell's Ferry. It took only a few more minutes after that to get the militia in sight.

Thomas sat behind Malcolm not saying a word, for fear he would turn back and dump him off at the Hutchinsons' front gate after all. Even at that, about a half mile after they caught sight of the militia, Malcolm said, *"Shhh!"*

"I didn't say anything!" Thomas whispered.

"Hush now! Did you hear that?"

"Hear what?" All Thomas could hear was the eerie, voiceless tramping of the soldiers ahead.

"Behind us," Malcolm hissed. "I thought I heard a horse. Look back!"

Thomas twisted his head around as far as he could and peered into the darkness. There was nothing but the skeleton shadows of the bare trees and his own icy breath fogging the air.

"I don't see a horse," he whispered. "Do you think someone followed us?"

"I don't know who would," Malcolm said. He shrugged. "I'm just imaginin' things. Must be the excitement."

Malcolm *was* excited. Thomas could feel it as he hung on behind him. His annoyance that Thomas was tagging along seemed to have drained from him, and his skin was shivering with more than the cold. He turned his head to the side so Thomas could see his square grin.

"We're going to see a real battle, Tireless!" he said.

"I know, Mighty," Thomas answered. "Is that why you wanted to come, just for the excitement?"

Malcolm shook his shaggy head. "I don't know why. This sounded like nonsense to me until I heard what Dr. Quincy said, then my heart just kept tellin' me I should be here. It's more than the adventure." He glanced over his shoulder at Thomas again. "Though I was becomin' afraid that I'd outgrown our adventures, you know?"

"Have you?" Thomas said.

Malcolm grinned. "We're havin' one now, aren't we?"

Thomas nodded. For this moment at least, he was happy.

They rode in silence for a long time, being careful to stay out of the sight of the militia, but always knowing just where it was. Finally, the band of soldiers seemed to be drawing to a halt, and Malcolm cut through a field on the side of the road to find a place to watch. As Malcolm guided Burgess through the shadows, Thomas kept his eye on the band of soldiers. They could get closer to them now that they were shielded by the trees, and Thomas picked out familiar figures in the dark—the men he'd watched for so many days, getting ready for this very night.

There was the leathersmith's son and one of Mr. Wetherburn's boys. Thomas Nelson himself, of course. And there was—

Thomas felt himself scowling. "There goes Xavier Wormeley," he whispered to Malcolm. He squinted through the darkness. "He has somebody by the arm already. Can't he go anywhere without forcing someone to do something?"

Malcolm nodded absently as he coaxed Burgess in under a stand of evergreens. The trees' pine needles shielded them from the lines of soldiers who were taking their places to block the road. "The British are expected anytime now," he said. "Thomas Nelson got word from one of the Patriot spies. I heard him talking in their headquarters at the courthouse when I went to deliver a letter for Clayton."

But Thomas stopped listening and stared at Xavier Wormeley and the figure he was shoving along in front of him. The man was tall, thin, and awkward as a farm boy going off to school in town.

"Malcolm!" Thomas squealed breathlessly.

"Keep your voice down, or I'll make you walk home."

"It's Nicholas!"

"What?"

"That's who Xavier is pushing—it's Dr. Quincy!"

Malcolm stood up in the stirrups and gave a long whistle under his breath. "So it is, lad," he said. "That bloated catfish is forcing him to serve after all!"

"They can't make him!"

"It looks like they're doing it," Malcolm said grimly.

"We have to stop them!"

"Not now." Malcolm cocked his head and slowly began to nod. "Do you hear that, lad? It's the British. They're comin'."

The words were barely out of his mouth before a ripple of excitement went through the militia, and even the soldiers' guns seemed to stiffen. Thomas wondered what the thundering noise was—and realized it was his own heart pounding furiously in his chest.

And then, out of the night, a herd of horses driven by men in tall hats rounded the bend. There was a moment of realization as the steeds slowed and danced uncertainly. Then someone shouted, "Fire!"

Suddenly, the night seemed to burst into flame. Muskets flared and then smoked and then flared again, ripping the air with their sharp retorts. Thomas flung his arms around Malcolm's waist and hung on as screams shrilled over the snapping of the weapons.

"Are the Patriots being shot?" Thomas cried. "Are they being killed?"

Malcolm's answer came out with a grunt of disgust. "No! They're runnin' away!"

Thomas squinted through the smoke and gasped. Malcolm was right. The Williamsburg militia had turned tail and was running in every direction—some back toward the town, others into the woods across the road, and still more right toward them.

"They can't do that!" Thomas cried. "They can't just . . . just run when the shooting starts!"

"They're doing it," Malcolm said, his voice laced with disappointment.

They both watched in disbelief as the "battlefield" emptied, leaving only the Patriot officers on their horses shouting and shooting their pistols into the air. The British, meanwhile, were trotting through as smoothly as a brook. Their laughter cut through the night—and through Thomas.

"I am ashamed to call myself a Patriot," Malcolm said angrily. "We could have done better ourselves, you and I. And Caroline and Patsy, too, for that matter!"

He picked up the reins and rode Burgess out into the clearing toward the road.

"Will they capture Williamsburg now?" Thomas asked.

Malcolm shook his head. "They've gotten all they want from Williamsburg. Most say they're headed for Portsmouth, where they can take the port and keep American supplies from coming in. Those soldiers of ours were supposed to keep at least this British company from doing that."

"Why are they so stupid?" Thomas asked. "Why did they run away like that?"

"They're not trained to be soldiers," he said. "They're just a bunch of farmers and shopkeepers with rifles."

"And no conscience," Thomas said.

They rode slowly and silently back toward town. The sounds of horses picking their way through the woods were everywhere, and occasionally they spotted someone cowering in the trees. Thomas wanted to shout at them, "Come out, coward!"

"Here's one limping along the road," Malcolm said. "They must have run over him trying to get away."

Thomas nodded, and then he felt his eyes bulge.

"Malcolm!" he cried. "That's Nicholas!"

"By heaven, you're right, lad!"

Malcolm dug his heels into Burgess and galloped up beside the tall doctor, who was staggering forlornly along the road. Thomas was on the ground before the horse stopped.

"Dr. Quincy! Are you all right?"

The face that looked back at him was pale and creased with pain, but Nicholas smiled with his eyes.

"What on earth are you doing here, Thomas?" he said. And then he shook his head. "It doesn't matter. I'm glad you are."

Malcolm joined them and pulled Nicholas's arm around his neck. Thomas did the same on the other side. The doctor leaned heavily on them both.

"What happened, sir?" Malcolm asked.

"I've been shot," Nicholas said.

Thomas looked at him in horror.

"Where?" Malcolm asked.

"In the upper part of my leg. I don't think it hit the bone. I tried to bandage it." He drew a rattled breath and smiled faintly. "I may need a doctor, though."

"We'll get you to Francis, sir," Malcolm said. "We'll put you right up on Burgess."

Nicholas nodded and murmured, "Thank you."

But Malcolm looked at Thomas, and his eyes said, "How are we going to do this?"

Thomas had no idea. His thoughts, his hammering heart, his terror were all swirling like a stirring soup. He tried to grab on to something.

"I'll hold Burgess steady!" he cried. "You help him on."

Malcolm tried, but Nicholas was too weak to pull himself up even with Malcolm pushing.

"What if I got on and pulled him up?" Thomas asked.

"I'll try anything," Malcolm said.

Thomas flung himself onto the horse's back and grabbed the arms Nicholas threw in his direction. He held on tight, but Malcolm couldn't get the lanky body past the stirrups.

"I have no strength," Nicholas said. "I'm sorry."

With that, his eyes rolled back into his head, and his weight sagged against Malcolm.

"He's fainting dead away!" Thomas cried. "Oh, please, God, what should we do?"

"Grab hold of his arms and pull!" Malcolm shouted.

Thomas did, and with one mighty heave, Malcolm shoved the doctor's body up onto the saddle. His head hung down on one side, his legs on the other.

"We have to hold that wounded leg up," Thomas said. "He always says that when there's bleeding."

"All right, then," Malcolm said. Thomas could hear the sob that threatened in his throat. "Can you climb down and hold it up while I lead the horse?"

"How will we keep him from falling off?" Thomas said as he slid off Burgess's flank.

"We'll pray," Malcolm said grimly.

And Thomas did as he walked beside Burgess and held Nicholas's leg up over his shoulder. *God, Father, please help us do the right thing. Please, please help us to find a way to get him home. Please, please don't let him die.*

"How goes it, lad?" Malcolm called back to him.

"I think he's sliding some!" Thomas said. "Can you stop?"

"I don't think we'd better. There's someone coming."

Thomas's mouth went dry. "Do you think it's the British?"

"I'm not takin' a chance. Let's get off into the trees."

"But what about Nicholas?"

"He'll be worse off if we're captured!"

"But—"

"Move!" Malcolm commanded him.

Thomas held tight to Nicholas's leg and trotted with the horse toward the trees. But they didn't move quickly enough. A horse's hooves drummed toward them faster than they could get out of sight.

"Whoa there!" a deep voice boomed at them.

"Don't stop, Thomas!" Malcolm whispered frantically.

Thomas had to grab Nicholas's legs with both arms and run sideways to keep up. A branch slapped him in the face, and his foot skidded across a patch of frozen mud, but he kept moving until the voice was suddenly on top of them, shouting, "Halt, I say!"

And a large horse cut in front of them.

✞ ✞ ✞

Chapter Seventeen

"**D**idn't you hear me calling to you, Thomas?" the man said.

Thomas looked over the top of Nicholas's legs, and his heart stopped.

"Papa!" he cried.

"Master Hutchinson, I beg your pardon, sir!" Malcolm stammered. "We were so busy tryin' to protect the doctor here—"

"Let's get him onto Judge," Papa said. "I can ride behind him, and he can lean on me."

"His leg needs to be up high, Papa," Thomas said.

"We can stretch it across the horse's neck."

They set about at once transferring Nicholas from Burgess's back to Judge's. This time it seemed as easy as moving a rag doll. Nicholas opened his eyes once and smiled gratefully at Papa.

"God always knows the right way, eh?" he said.

He closed his eyes again, but Thomas could tell he was still with them. It was as if everything were going to be all right now—now that Papa was here.

It wasn't until he was back on Burgess with Malcolm that the fear started lapping at Thomas's insides again. His father hadn't said a word about him and Malcolm being out there in the middle of the night or what he was going to do about it. But it was coming—that was sure. There was no use even praying about that.

Malcolm, however, had a different comment.

"Your father wasn't surprised to come upon us," he said. "It was as if he were out looking for us."

Thomas nodded miserably. "He must have come home from the plantation tonight and found us and Burgess gone and—"

"But he seemed to expect to find us with Nicholas," Malcolm insisted. "He seemed to know the whole story."

Thomas shrugged. "It doesn't matter. I'm in trouble no matter what."

Malcolm looked at him sideways. "Even though you risked your life to save the doctor?"

"I did?"

"Don't be an idiot. Of course you did!"

"But that's not why we came out here in the first place."

Malcolm shook his head. "I think that's why I came out here, only I didn't know it."

"Your conscience?" Thomas said.

"God," Malcolm said.

When they reached the Hutchinsons' house just behind Papa and Nicholas, the place was ablaze with candles and a fire in the parlor fireplace. For the third time in a very short while, a patient was unloaded onto the sofa, and Otis and Esther scurried around with firewood and tea.

Francis was already there, too, with the medicines he needed dug out of the straw. Mama, with a wrap around her nightshift, seemed to be directing the entire operation.

"We'll need more blankets, Malcolm," she said. "There are some in the spare bedroom upstairs."

Malcolm nodded and took off.

"Hutchinson! Over here, boy!" Francis barked. "Hold this basin while I remove the bullet. You're a fortunate man, Nicholas. It's just beneath the skin."

For a moment, Thomas stared at the wound.

"What are you gawkin' at, boy?" Francis said. "You've seen bullet wounds before."

"It's in the front," Thomas said.

"You get brighter every day," Francis muttered as he went to work. "We can all see it's in the front."

"You didn't run," Thomas said softly to Nicholas.

Dr. Quincy opened his eyes, which by now were almost without any color at all. "It's not fear that keeps me out of war," he said. "It's God. There was no need to run away."

"Tell that to the 400 men who scattered like a bunch of sheep!" Papa said. "I am as disappointed as I have ever been. I don't know what to do now."

"We could start by praying."

Thomas didn't look up because he had to hold the basin

steady for Francis to drop the unexploded musket ball into it. But he knew it was Clayton who had spoken. His big brother was already murmuring softly under his breath, and then a bell-like voice was praying softly with him. Soon a deep voice joined in, and there was a trio of prayers filling the room. Thomas saw the chills go up his arm in little bumps.

"Thank you, God," Nicholas sighed.

It didn't take long for Francis and Thomas to get Nicholas bandaged up and off to sleep. Everyone else gathered around the table in front of the fire and talked in hushed voices as they sipped cups of lemon balm tea. Otis hovered at the woodpile in the corner, and Esther circled the table, keeping the cups filled. But Papa insisted that Malcolm sit with them—so they could sort things out, he said.

Here it comes, Thomas thought. *I'm sure to get my ears boxed now—or worse.*

"I was on my way home from the plantation when a horse flew out of the woods as if it had wings, and the young boy on it shouted for me to stop. Strange young man. I could never see his face, he was so bundled up. But it must be someone you know," he added to Thomas, "because he called you by name. He said you and Malcolm had found Dr. Quincy wounded and were trying to bring him back to town by yourselves. He said you needed my help."

"We did," Malcolm said ruefully.

"I'm not so sure of that," Papa said. "You would have made it back the way you were going, though surely not as fast." He surveyed them both from under his thick, dusty eyebrows. "It's a wonder that you were able to get him up onto the horse like that. He's a handful, even though he's so slender."

"I don't know, sir," Malcolm said. "I just had a rush of fear, and suddenly he was on the horse. They say fear gives you strength. I once saw a man—"

Thomas rolled his eyes.

"I tend to think it's God who gives you strength in such situations," Clayton said.

Thomas looked curiously at his brother. It didn't sound like an answer he'd gotten by pulling a handle. And somehow, he wanted to hear more.

"Sir," Malcolm said. "I know you will want to hear why Thomas and I were at Burwell's Ferry tonight, and I first want to apologize for—"

"For what?" Papa said. "Yes, I am still the head of this household, but it seems to me that some very wise decisions are being made in my absence. My wife has every woman in town praying and rolling bandages and who knows what all else, and she conducts a sickroom like a general. Thomas here—and you, Malcolm—are running a successful apothecary shop out of my stable. And Clayton is not only seeing to the spiritual needs of the entire household, but he is keeping the town honest about theirs as well."

Papa was met with a room full of blank faces.

"Didn't you know," he continued, "that it was Clayton who found the right people to send a direct order to the Williamsburg militia that Dr. Nicholas Quincy, and any other godly man who did not want to serve, was to be released at once under Virginia law?"

"Clayton, why didn't you tell us?" Mama cried.

"How did you manage it?" Francis said. "I've been shouting at Xavier Wormeley for months, and it's done me no good!"

Thomas already knew how Clayton would answer that one. He would say he just listened to God and did what He said.

Papa leaned back in his chair and stretched his big arms wearily. "I have only one complaint," he said.

"What is that, my dear?" Mama said anxiously.

"Thomas—"

Thomas let his teacup clatter to the saucer. "Yes, sir?"

"I have no quarrel with your dashing off on a horse in your condition. Heaven knows I did the same thing myself." He nodded at Thomas's bruised eyes. "But no one has told me how you got into such a state. I can only assume you were fighting."

"Sir, may I?" Malcolm said before Thomas could open his mouth.

Papa nodded impatiently. *"Someone* tell me!"

"I witnessed the attack, sir," he said. "It was three boys who jumped on him. The lad here did none of the fightin'."

Papa's eyebrows shot up like two arrows. "Three boys? In heaven's name, why?"

All eyes turned to Thomas. He looked helplessly around the table, and his eyes stopped at Clayton. His brother nodded at him.

"They are in my class at the grammar school," Thomas said. "They took a dislike to me from the start, even before the school opened, when they threw a rock and hit Caroline Taylor in the head. And then when you put their fathers in their places at Wetherburn's Tavern that Sunday, they hated me sure."

"Go on," Papa said.

"They could never recite correctly in class, but I could. Master Wrigley would snap his whip at them and call them idiots. They warned me if I ever showed them up again, I would be sorry."

"And did you?" Papa said.

"Yes, sir."

"And are you? Sorry, I mean?"

"No, sir."

"Why not?"

Thomas's eyes sprang open. "Why not, sir?"

"Well, you were beaten within an inch of your life. Wouldn't it have been easier to play the dunce in school?"

"It would have been wrong!"

"Ah, so it's better to be right and bruised than wrong and safe."

Thomas tripped over that one. "I . . . I suppose so, sir."

"You suppose correctly," Papa said. "You and Dr. Quincy and Francis Pickering—and every other Patriot in this room. You're all correct about that. You've fought the battle well in my absence, and I'm proud of the lot of you."

Clayton cleared his throat. "I can only speak for myself, of course, but I believe each of us has done it with God's help."

Everyone nodded—except Thomas. That didn't escape Papa.

"You seem to have some doubt about that, Thomas," John Hutchinson said.

Thomas felt his face go scarlet, and he looked at his lap.

"Thomas," Papa said in his warning voice.

"I told God. I told Him what I wanted, and I asked Him for it!" Thomas blurted out. "But those boys still beat me up—and Nicholas was still put in jail—and Caroline still hates me for being a Patriot!"

Papa watched him struggle for a moment, and then he turned to Clayton.

"You are the minister in our family," he said. "Would you care to address this?"

Clayton sat up straight in the chair, and Thomas gnawed at his mouth to keep from shouting, "Please don't give me a sermon!"

"I used to do what you've done, Thomas," Clayton said—in an unsermon-like voice. "I read my prayers out of the prayer book like a dutiful Christian, but when it came to my own prayers, I was forever telling God what I wanted and what I needed." He shook his head sheepishly. "It wasn't until I found that I had to act as Papa would that I saw my mistake."

He stopped. Malcolm leaned forward earnestly. "What was it?" he said.

"God doesn't take directions," Clayton said. "He gives them. Our job is to ask for help and then take it. I see the war this way, in fact. We are fighting for the right to do what God would have us do. That was why I couldn't let

Nicholas rot in jail and why I cannot let Xavier Wormeley get away with what he did tonight." He glanced toward the sofa. "If Nicholas had been killed, I would have had Mr. Wormeley hanged for murder!"

"Do you understand that, Thomas?" Papa said.

Thomas wasn't the only one in the room who nodded.

"Now then," John Hutchinson said, "there is one more matter to be addressed here. Thomas, did you pray to God to take you out of that school?"

"Yes, sir," Thomas admitted.

"Then that is one 'direction' that God has followed. I will not have you studying with a teacher who waves a whip at students and calls them idiots. Or who accuses my son of cheating."

"Cheating!" Mama cried.

"I received a message from Master Wrigley—all the way out at the homestead, mind you—telling me that Thomas had received a perfect score on an examination, and that surely he had cheated somehow."

"Nonsense!" Clayton cried. "I questioned him on that material myself. He knew it inside out, and he'd learned it from Alexander Taylor, not this Master Wiggly or whatever his name is."

Thomas couldn't hold back a guffaw.

"Then there is no need at all for you to return to that classroom," John Hutchinson said. "We will make other arrangements for your education until the war is over and the college returns to its high quality of instruction."

"Thank goodness for that," Francis said. "I hope this

means he can return to work for me, John. Nicholas and I, we need the boy."

Thomas stared at him. Just a few weeks ago, he'd told Thomas he was just "underfoot" in the apothecary shop. Why—?

But he knew why. Francis had been trying to go along with Papa's wishes.

It's good to obey Papa, Thomas thought. *But when he isn't here, we do pretty well on our own, don't we? We— and God.*

"I have a question!" Esther said boldly, and then looked quickly at Papa. "If I may, sir?"

Papa smiled a half smile. "Is there any hope of my stopping you, Esther?"

Esther didn't answer but plunged on. "I would like to know what is to become of the three boys who brought our Thomas to the brink of death? I was assured that you would handle it."

"And I will," John Hutchinson said.

Thomas squirmed a little in his seat. Papa was taking him out of school. Papa was going to see that the boys were punished and never bothered him again. Papa was doing it all, and now that didn't set right with—

With what? he asked himself.

With my conscience, he answered.

He looked up to find Malcolm watching him. His eyes were burning.

"Sir?" Thomas said to his father.

Papa nodded.

"May I be the one to . . . to handle the boys?"

"John, no!" Mama cried. "He was nearly killed last time!"

Francis wheezed loudly. "It wasn't as bad as all that," he said.

"Handle it how, Thomas?" Papa said.

"I won't fight them," Thomas said, "I will . . . I don't know yet." He took a deep breath and lifted his chin. "I'll have to talk to God first."

Papa thought for a moment, and then he nodded. Mama gasped, but he put his hand on hers.

"One try without fighting," he said to Thomas. "If it appears not to work, you must tell me immediately, and I will take over. Agreed?"

"Yes, sir!" he said.

And then he looked at Malcolm. He could already see a plan taking shape in his black eyes.

✝ ✦ ✝

Chapter Eighteen

It was late the next day before Thomas found Malcolm alone. Thomas had just been sent to Francis's with a delivery of some of their "stable medicine." When he came back to the stable to be sure he'd covered up the other herbs safely, the servant boy was waiting for him—feet propped up on Burgess's stall, arms crossed, eyes sparkling.

"It's time we talked about how to 'handle' those three bullies," Malcolm said.

Thomas burrowed down into the straw beside him and hugged his jacket close. "You want to help me, then?"

Malcolm cocked one shaggy eyebrow. "Do these horses have manes?"

"Well, yes."

"*Of course* I want to help! I was the first one who saw what they did to you, lad. Remember? We can't let them get away with that."

Thomas looked into his sharp eyes. "You have a plan already, don't you?"

Malcolm cocked the other eyebrow.

"It can't include beating them up," Thomas cautioned.

Both eyebrows went up this time, and the square smile came with it. "But they don't have to know that, now, do they?"

There was a crafty sound to his voice, and Thomas couldn't help leaning in to listen. Malcolm was only two steps into the plan when he stopped and put his finger to his lips.

"What is it?" Thomas whispered.

Malcolm pointed toward the side of the stable that faced the Palace Green and mouthed the word "listen."

Thomas did, and for a moment he didn't hear anything. And then he heard whispering under the stable window.

Malcolm put his mouth close to Thomas's ear. "You were followed from Mr. Pickering's. It's those same people, I bet. We have to catch them, or our whole plan could be spoiled."

"You think it's them? Zachary and the others?"

Malcolm frowned. "We have to find out, eh?"

Thomas nodded.

"So, lad!" Malcolm said then—loudly enough to be heard in Yorktown. "Let's go to the kitchen and finish this conversation, eh?"

He nodded impatiently at Thomas.

"Are you sure we won't be overheard there?" Thomas said—even louder.

Malcolm grinned. "Not a chance!"

Malcolm led the way to the door, being careful to knock over an oat bucket and stomp his feet en route. He opened the door and then slammed it firmly. They waited inside the stable—and sure enough, the gate creaked open, and they heard footsteps outside. They waited until the footsteps reached the kitchen building before Malcolm opened the stable door a crack and peeked out.

Thomas wriggled in beside him. "Who is it?" he whispered.

Malcolm turned and looked at him with his mouth hanging open. "You won't believe it, lad!" he whispered. "Look for yourself!"

Thomas peered through the crack and gasped. It was Patsy and Caroline, standing with their backs to the stable, peering into the kitchen window.

"What?" Thomas whispered.

"Let's get them!" Malcolm said.

He flung open the stable door, and with a roar and three leaps, he had his little sister up on his shoulders. Thomas flew at Caroline and turned her around by the shoulders.

And then he didn't know what to do. He wanted to laugh and shout, "You thought you could outsmart us, eh? No such luck!"

And she looked as if she wanted to say, "We did, Tom Hutchinson! And don't you forget it!"

But neither of them said anything. They only looked at each other—sadly. And then Caroline wrenched her shoulders away.

"You!" Thomas said finally.

"Yes, us," Caroline said. She straightened the folds of her red capuchin as if she hadn't a care in the world.

"It's been you all along, then!" said Malcolm. Patsy was pulling his hair from her position across his back, but he was ignoring her. "That day we were going to the jail, the night we went to Burwell's Ferry—"

"And a good thing for you, too," Caroline said. She tossed her hood off. "If it weren't for us spying on you, those bullies would have broken Thomas's leg. Right, Patsy?"

Patsy nodded and gave Malcolm's hair a yank.

"And you surely wouldn't have gotten Nicholas back here if I hadn't seen you trying to get him on your horse and gone for your Papa."

Malcolm pulled Patsy's face down by one braid to look at her. "You rode to Burwell's Ferry?"

She grinned.

"Why did you spy on us?" Malcolm said.

Caroline's haughty air disappeared, and she began to make circles on the ground with the toe of her boot. "You wouldn't let me be a part of things anymore, so I had to find my own way." She looked up anxiously at Malcolm. "Patsy wanted to help me," she said. "I didn't make her!"

Malcolm snorted. "No one makes my sister do anything."

Patsy pinched his nose happily from behind.

But Thomas wasn't happy. He looked miserably at Caroline. "What do you mean, we wouldn't let you be a part of things?"

She looked back just as miserably. "You didn't let us help you move Francis's medicines or hunt for Nicholas or—"

"You went away mad—"

"Because you treated me as if I were the enemy! And I'm not, Tom Hutchinson! I don't care about the silly war. I don't care what the British do or what side Alexander is on. I just want to be your friend!"

There was a stunned silence. Caroline rubbed her tears with the backs of her hands. Thomas tried to catch one of his spinning thoughts—any one.

"You want to be my friend? Still?" he said finally. "Even though your father let the British officers stay in his house?"

"I'd stop there if I were you, lad," Malcolm said between his teeth.

"They made Papa do that!" Caroline cried. "They said they'd hurt Mama and me if he didn't give them beds to sleep in! We all spent the night in the kitchen so we wouldn't have to be with those miserable men! My father doesn't believe in forcing people. It's against his—"

"Conscience," Malcolm finished for her.

She nodded and went to work on the tears again. Thomas tried to find a better thought this time.

"Why didn't you tell me, then, instead of storming out of the kitchen that day like you hated me?"

"Because you looked like you hated me," she said. "Because Alexander is still a Loyalist and because Papa told the British about Francis and Nicholas—while they were pointing a pistol at him, I might add!"

Thomas stared. "You didn't tell me that part!"

"You didn't listen! You never do—"

"It's you who never listens! I tried to—"

A whistle blasted between them. Thomas jumped and looked up to see Patsy, still on her brother's back, holding her ears. Malcolm removed his fingers from his mouth.

"We don't have time for all this," he said. "We've a plan to make. Now give each other a hug, and let's get on with it, eh?"

Caroline swept her cape around her. "I will not hug him!" she said haughtily.

Thomas caught his breath.

And then she smiled—her slice-of-melon smile. "He's a boy!" she said.

"Wouldn't hug you if you paid me," Thomas said, smothering his smile.

Malcolm nodded toward the stable. "Then let's go and get busy, eh?"

The next day was a perfect one for carrying out "The Plan." The sun cut through the chill of a hurt-your-eyes blue sky, and there was even the hint of spring in the air. Thomas was glad not to have to put on so many clothes. It would be easier to move around this way, and there would be a lot of moving around to do.

It was hard to wait until eleven o'clock, when he knew the Terrible Trio would be coming out of school for dinner. And it was even harder to cross the Palace Green toward the college without the rest of the Fearsome Foursome at his side. He tried not to glance behind him to be sure they were sneaking along behind him.

I just have to know they're there, he told himself.

And he knew they were. After all, they'd all prayed together in the stable last night, puffing out frosty air and asking God to please give them direction. Malcolm had explained all about conscience, and the girls had caught on right away.

So Thomas kept his eyes straight ahead and didn't even look around when he reached a stand of pine trees in the college yard and slipped behind it.

The yard just beyond the trees was suddenly alive with boys' voices, and Thomas listened over them. There it was, Malcolm's whistle, telling him the Terrible Trio was approaching. Thomas said one more prayer, took a deep breath, and stepped out, right into their path.

For an instant they all looked as if they wanted to bolt— Yancy most of all.

But Zachary recovered himself quickly and said, "Well, well, look who's here! Idiot Hutchinson."

"My friends call me Tom," Thomas said calmly. "You can call me Thomas." That had been Caroline's idea. He liked the look it brought to their faces.

Zachary took a step forward. "It seems you've grown smarter since we last saw you. But not quite smart enough, eh, boys?"

Kent and Yancy dutifully shook their heads.

"If you were really smart," Zachary went on, "you'd already be running, because we're going to get you—again!"

But Thomas didn't run. And he didn't double up his fists. Zachary looked startled.

"You want to fight?" Thomas said.

Zachary gave a hard laugh. "If you want to call it that! I call it beating the tar out of you. And you can't do a thing—"

"Well," Thomas said, "if that's the only way you know of handling things, I suppose that will have to do. But I *have* gotten smarter."

He put up his hand and waved it in the air. From out of nowhere, a wiry, shaggy-haired young man appeared and came to stand beside Thomas.

"This is my friend Malcolm," Thomas said. "He's here to make this an even fight."

Zachary tried to laugh again, but there seemed to be something caught in his throat. "This isn't even," he said cautiously. "There are three of us and only two of you."

"But *which* two?" Thomas said. "That's the important thing. Malcolm."

Malcolm stepped forward until he was nose to nose with Zachary. There was no trace of the square smile. It had been replaced by a pair of glittering, narrowed eyes that would have frightened a bear.

"Malcolm here can take two of you, and with my help all three of you will go down," Thomas said calmly. "But I don't really want to fight. It goes against my conscience."

"Your *what?*" Yancy said.

Zachary jabbed him with an elbow. "You're a coward, then?" he said to Thomas.

"No. I'm a scholar. I just want to get my education and not be disturbed by people like you."

In devising the plan, Malcolm had wanted him to say idiots, but Caroline had put her foot down.

"So," Thomas went on, "if you see me on the street, I want you to leave me alone. I won't be bullied anymore."

The Terrible Trio was frozen to the ground. They stared in disbelief as Malcolm and Thomas turned on their heels and walked slowly away and around the corner out of their sight, staying close to the hedge. Thomas couldn't stand it any longer. He had to ask.

"Can we follow through on that if we have to?" he whispered.

Malcolm nodded. "Everything is ready, lad," he whispered back.

For a few steps, it looked as if Zachary, Kent, and Yancy were going to take Thomas's advice and go their way. But Zachary suddenly burst out, "Get 'em, boys!"

Before they could get around the corner, Malcolm grabbed Thomas's arm and pulled him behind the hedge.

There were two buckets there. Thomas smelled them before he saw them, and he wrinkled his nose.

"They're the worst Francis could concoct," Caroline said. Patsy nodded.

"I can tell," Thomas said.

Malcolm grinned his square smile and held out his arms to hug them all. "All right, then, Fearsome Foursome," he whispered. "The time has come."

Patsy and Caroline nodded, and Caroline jumped out onto the street with her basket in her hand.

✛ ⋅✛⋅ ✛

Chapter Nineteen

Thomas peeked through the hedge in time to see Zachary skid to a halt and look down, mystified, at the little girl who looked back up at him. Thomas had to cover his mouth to keep from laughing at the innocence on her face.

"Move aside!" Zachary said to her.

"Yes, do!" Kent chimed in.

Yancy, of course, nodded until his ears wiggled.

"Are you looking for Thomas Hutchinson?" Caroline asked.

Zachary looked at her sharply. "Yes. Do you know where he is?"

"I do," she said.

Thomas could see the thousand dimples appearing in each cheek.

"Well, tell me!" Zachary cried. His lip was curled back over his gapped teeth.

"Oh," Caroline said. "You didn't say you wanted to know."

"I *did!* Where is he?"

"I believe he's behind that hedge there," she said.

"That's our cue," Malcolm whispered.

Thomas turned and took the bucket Patsy handed him, and Malcolm did the same. He held his breath against the smell and waited.

"You'd better be telling the truth, girl!" Zachary said.

"Or what?" Caroline said sweetly. "You'll beat me up the way you did him?"

"He told you?" Kent said.

But Zachary said, "Shut it, fool!" and then shouted into the hedge, "Hutchinson, if you're in there, come out now. You'll regret it if I have to come in after you."

Thomas looked at Malcolm, who nodded. Thomas stood up, keeping the bucket low.

"Did you call me?" he said.

"Coward!" Zachary cried. "Come out and fight!"

"All right," Thomas said. And he raised the bucket and dumped its gooey, sticky, smelly contents directly on Kent's head.

"My turn!" Malcolm cried. He popped up next to Thomas and plunked his bucket upside down on Yancy's head.

Thomas would have loved to have reveled in the shouts of horror and disgust that came from under those buckets, but he knew what was coming next, and he didn't want to miss it.

"What do you think you're doing, Hutchinson!" Zachary

screamed, his eyes watering from the smell.

"Do you feel left out, Zachary?" Thomas said. "Please don't. We have something special for you."

Caroline tapped Zachary on the shoulder, and he turned irritably.

"What?" he said.

She smiled and pulled the cover off her basket. "Go Martha," she said softly.

Martha needed no more of an invitation than that. She let out one long warning hiss before she smacked her paw at Zachary's arm.

"Ow!" he cried and hunched over, holding his arm against his side.

"Martha, how rude!" Caroline said, smiling her slice-of-melon smile. "Now say you're sorry!"

She pulled Martha from the basket and plopped her on Zachary's shoulder. The claws came out and dragged all the way down his arm. Zachary sent up a howl that Thomas was sure could be heard down at Francis's apothecary. Zachary took off at a dead run, batting the snarling Martha off with both hands.

Meanwhile, only Kent had been able to pull the bucket from his head, and he took off after his leader. Poor Yancy was still tugging and turning himself in a circle.

"Let me help you with that," Malcolm said. He pulled the bucket off and steered Yancy in the direction of his friends. "They went that way," he said.

"Zachary!" Yancy screeched and stumbled off down the street.

"Are you sure that stuff won't hurt them?" Thomas said.

"Francis says it will just make them smell foul for a while," Caroline said.

"As far as I'm concerned, they've always smelled foul," Malcolm said. "Besides, Francis put in another wee surprise for good measure."

Thomas felt his face pucker. "What surprise?"

"That wonderful concoction has a good dose of indigo in it. Their hair will be blue for months!"

Caroline erupted into giggles.

"They won't poke their heads out of their houses," Malcolm continued, "and I say good riddance."

But suddenly, Patsy tugged at his sleeve. "Not yet, Malcolm," she said. "That one with the ugly lip is coming back!"

Zachary was indeed headed back toward him, nursing his scratched arm with his other hand and obviously ready to continue the fight.

"He's a stubborn one, isn't he?" Malcolm said. "You know the final step, lad?"

Thomas nodded and stepped out to meet Zachary.

"Be careful, Tom," Caroline whispered.

Thomas took a deep breath. He'd been saving this piece of information, and he hoped it worked. *Please, God,* he started to pray. But he knew it would work. It was the right thing to do. God, in His way, had told him.

"You've not heard the last of me, Hutchinson!" Zachary screamed at him. His lip had all but disappeared. "You may have run away from the school like a sissy ninny, but you can't run away from me! I will get you someday when you don't have your friends with you!"

"Will you?" Thomas said. "Then I suppose you haven't heard the last of me either."

Zachary narrowed his eyes.

"If you ever try to attack me again—with words or with fists—I will have to tell what I know."

Zachary's shoulders drooped a bit. "And what is that?" he said.

"I haven't told anyone, except my friends here, that you tried to make me cheat. But if you even threaten me again, I will."

There was a stung silence before Zachary forced himself to laugh. "No one will believe you!"

"My father will," Thomas said. "And I will have to let him take care of it after that."

"This is a bluff!"

"There is only one way to find out if it is," Malcolm said. "But I warn you, you won't get far."

Zachary doubled up his fists and waved them at his sides. The Foursome stood and looked at him without flinching.

The arms flopped to Zachary's sides, leaving only his lip curled. When he finally spoke, his voice was dead. "I hate you, Hutchinson."

They all watched him hurry off down the street.

"Have we seen the last of him?" Patsy said anxiously.

"I think so, lass," Malcolm said.

"Well, Tom," Caroline said as they walked home together while Malcolm went to deliver Patsy to Lydia's. "What's our next adventure?"

"I'm tired of adventures!" Thomas wailed. "I've had enough of them lately."

"The only reason you're tired of adventures is because you haven't had one with me in a long time," she said. She grinned at him sideways. "And you must, because I'm your partner."

Thomas kicked at a loose stone. "But what if . . . ?"

"What if what?"

"What if we find out that Alexander is . . . ? What if he's . . . ?"

"You mean a Patriot?" she said.

"Yes."

She swept her red capuchin around her. "Our brothers can do what they want, but I'm never going to let them or the war or anything else come between us again." She looked him full in the face. "Are you?"

Thomas searched his conscience, but it only took a second to find the answer. "No," he said.

"Good," she said. "Now I'm going home, because I think it's high time we *had* an adventure. I'm going to get ready."

"What are you talking about?" Thomas said.

Her brown eyes shined, and the dimples took over her cheeks. "Well, if I told you, it wouldn't be an adventure now, would it?"

When she was gone, Thomas went home to an afternoon-quiet house. The only voices he heard when he came in the back door were from Papa's library.

"Is that you, Thomas?" Papa called.

"Yes, sir."

"Good! Why don't you join us?"

Thomas smelled hot apple cider as he walked in, and Clayton was already pouring him a tankard full.

"We are having a small celebration," Papa said. His usually piercing eyes were easy. "Your mother has taught us how important these little parties are, eh?"

"What are we celebrating?" Thomas asked.

"I have been blind these past months, Thomas," Papa said. "I failed to see that your brother Clayton has a calling that goes beyond my worries about smallpox and other such things."

Thomas blinked at him through the steam of his cider.

"He has run this household like a true man of God in my absence, praying his way through every difficulty and leading the rest of you. Why, your mother followed his example, and look at the ladies who meet in this house twice a week to pray and minister to the townspeople." Papa's eyes grew soft as he looked at Clayton. "A man like that must be ordained."

Thomas could feel his own eyes widening, and he looked at Clayton. There was a spot of color in each of his brother's pale cheeks, and he nodded shyly.

"The final piece came to me this morning when Nicholas Quincy arrived with the news that a doctor in Massachusetts has discovered a smallpox vaccine. As soon as Nicholas is able to obtain an inoculation for him, Clayton will be on his way to England."

Thomas didn't know what to say. He knew he had never seen his oldest brother look so completely peaceful. But Thomas himself felt suddenly empty. It was as if he and Clayton had just begun to discover each other, in their unspoken way. And now he, too, was going away. Thomas looked sadly into his cider.

"We shall have to write each other letters," Clayton said.

Thomas glanced up quickly.

"You're a fine scholar. I know you'll be a fine letter writer, too."

He smiled his faint smile. Thomas smiled back.

"Ah, and speaking of letters," Papa said, "we have received another from your brother Sam."

Thomas felt his ears almost pointing to attention.

Papa chuckled. "I would read it to you, but your mother has tucked it under her pillow to sleep on it."

"What did it say, sir?" Thomas asked, trying not to sound impatient.

"He's well, Thomas," Papa said. "And he is doing us all proud." He poured himself some more cider from the square pot and considered his cup for a moment.

"I'm afraid I have some unfortunate news as well. I might as well break it to you now, as long as we three are together."

Thomas stirred uneasily.

"Benedict Arnold has taken his men to Portsmouth— just miles from here—to set up his headquarters and keep the Patriots from receiving supplies by sea."

"We knew that was going to happen, didn't we, Father?" Clayton said.

Papa nodded, his face tight. "But what we didn't know is that Alexander Taylor has been seen at the British head-quarters there."

Thomas's heart turned to ice.

"It's true, then," Clayton said sadly. "He is on the side of the British."

"I'm afraid so."

Thomas stared into his cider. *Alexander is the enemy now,* he thought miserably. *He's not like Caroline. He lied to me—and to Sam. He's fighting for the other side.* The thoughts rammed into each other until Thomas's head ached. *Is this what he thinks is right? Is he doing this the way Sam is fighting for the Patriots and Nicholas won't fight for anyone?*

Thomas felt a hand on his shoulder. "Speak, son," Papa said. "Or your head will surely explode."

Thomas wasn't sure he could speak with the tears clogging his throat the way they were. But he swallowed and tried.

"Alexander always said he did what he believed . . . but what if he believes wrong?"

Clayton cleared his throat. "If I may, Father?"

Papa nodded.

"Perhaps the real question, Thomas," Clayton said, "is did Alexander go to God to find out what was right for him to believe?"

"That's always the long and the short of it, isn't it?" Papa said. He gave Thomas's shoulder a squeeze. "I know it's hard to believe this, what with all the fighting, even among our own friends, but if *you* go to God and take His direction, *you* will know what's best to do. And that is all any of us can do." He let go of Thomas's shoulder and went to the window. Clayton closed his eyes. It was as if they were giving him time to soak that in.

He did drink in the words, and they scared him a little. *I can count only on God, and me, and no one else?* he wondered. It felt lonely.

"Well!" Papa said suddenly. He turned to Thomas with his deep-set blue eyes twinkling. "We have a visitor, and I'm fairly certain the boy's here for you, Thomas."

Thomas hurried curiously to the window. Just as he got there, a figure in too-big breeches and a black cap darted from behind the bare oak tree to the hedge that lined the front walk. He turned his head to look around, and Thomas choked back a laugh.

The figure was wearing a mask.

"You're right, sir," Thomas said. "He's here for me."

Papa nodded, and Thomas tore for the door. Just as he opened it, Papa said, "Oh, Thomas, thank him for me—for coming to fetch me the night Nicholas was wounded."

Thomas whirled around to stare.

"He was brave that night," Papa said. And then his mouth twitched at the corners. "Or is it she?"

Thomas grinned and ran for the front door. It was *she* all right, and she was one person God had sent for him to have adventures with—and to depend on.

And even with the war raging closer and the sides always changing, he didn't feel lonely at all.

✠ ⦾ ✠